"AN ENGROSSING STORY."

—*Booklist*

"Brancato can write a scene that you have to believe, her teens have more mettle than most . . . and what's more, Jane Ann's conflict comes across as a real, involving dilemma."

—*Kirkus Reviews*

"I am glad to report that I have found a book that I can heartily recommend . . . This easy-reading narrative is a 'now' book dealing with the young's emotional experiences and disappointments. The ending will leave a lump in your throat."

—*Philadelphia Inquirer*

"Will leave sensitive readers shaken and moved. Throughout the plot, an astrological theme recurs—a deft touch, denoting the adolescent's desperate search for meaningful guidance."

—*Publishers Weekly*

Bantam Books by Robin F. Brancato

SOMETHING LEFT TO LOSE
WINNING

SOMETHING LEFT TO LOSE

by Robin F. Brancato

The characters in this novel are purely fictional. Any resemblance between them and persons living or dead is unintentional and coincidental.

This low-priced Bantam Book
has been completely reset in a type face
designed for easy reading, and was printed
from new plates. It contains the complete
text of the original hard-cover edition.
NOT ONE WORD HAS BEEN OMITTED.

SOMETHING LEFT TO LOSE
A Bantam Book / published by arrangement with
Alfred A. Knopf, Inc.

PRINTING HISTORY
Alfred A. Knopf edition published February 1976
Bantam edition / February 1979

Bantam Books are published by Bantam Books, Inc. Its trademark, consisting of the words "Bantam Books" and the por-
trayal of a bantam, is Registered in U.S. Patent and Trademark
Office and in other countries. Marca Registrada. Bantam
Books, Inc., 666 Fifth Avenue, New York, New York 10019.

PRINTED IN THE UNITED STATES OF AMERICA

For my mother and father

1

Jane Ann clamped her hand over her mouth to make sure she wouldn't laugh out loud. Lydia's elbow was jabbing her on one side, and on the other side she could feel Rebbie's whole body rumbling like a volcano.

"Reb, *if you make me laugh* . . ." Jane Ann said through clenched fingers. She pulled away from Rebbie and Lydia and raised herself just high enough to look over the top of the hedge. Luckily it was almost dark. Mr. Turner wouldn't recognize them right away, even if he heard strange noises in his yard. The only thing she could hear now, except for Rebbie's muffled laughter, was the rustle of leaves blowing along the sidewalk that led to the Turners' front porch forty feet in front of them.

"Jane Ann, I've got to sneeze." Lydia buried her face too late. "Ah-choo!"

Rebbie shouted louder than the sneeze, *"Gesundheit!"*

A light on the porch went on. Jane Ann ducked. "You nut, Rebbie!" she said. "You traitor! You made me come here—*now* look. He's going to see us!" She fixed her eyes on the front door.

Rebbie watched. "Nothing's happening," she said finally. "Relax. He doesn't know we're here. The light's just a coincidence."

The three of them stared over the hedge at the outline of the house. Nice place, Jane Ann thought, even though she couldn't relax. Stone-and-frame front; indoor and outdoor shutters;

porch with an old coach seat for a bench. Mr.
Turner liked antiques; he was always bringing
some interesting old thing to class. Through the
window she saw a light go on in what must be the
living room. Mr. Turner—and *his wife*—were
probably both at home. Jane Ann had been dying
to see where he lived since the first day of English class in September. She'd been dying to see
what his wife looked like. Now, forgetting all
about being caught in the act, she concentrated
for a minute on preserving details in her memory
as if they were flowers she was pressing in a
book: an apple tree in the Turners' side yard, its
fruit scattered on the ground; the October remnant of a rose garden; Mr. Turner's Volkswagen
in the driveway.

"O.K." Rebbie stood up. "Let's get moving."
Her form loomed above the hedge; her hair blew
out into a frizzy halo. Against the backdrop of
sky, Lydia's white face was a cameo. Lydia got up
on her knees.

"Wait," Jane Ann said. "Hold it." Suddenly the
possibility of being seen made her go weak. If
there was anybody in the world she didn't feel like
making a fool of herself in front of, it was Mr.
Turner. She grabbed Lydia's arm. "Lyddy, at
least *you're* sensible. Let's forget the whole
thing—please. Let's go home. My mother told me
six o'clock and it's six thirty now. She'll kill me."

"Go home?" Rebbie said.

Why did Rebbie's voice always blast out like a
foghorn? *A little sense, Reb,* Jane Ann thought. *A
little control!* The whole neighborhood didn't need
to know that three moronic girls were spying on
Hugh Turner.

"Did you say *go home?*" Rebbie asked.

Jane Ann hesitated. "It's just—it's just that
this is so childish," she said in a low voice. "I
mean, we're almost fifteen years old. Rebbie, you
are fifteen. Don't you feel dumb? He'll *see* us!"

Rebbie's hands were on her hips. "I thought you wanted the part in the play," she said.

"I do, but—"

"Then let's do what we have to."

Jane Ann sank back against the hedge, surprised at how close she was to crying. "I want the part," she said shakily, "but this is crazy. It's dark. My parents'll be mad. Besides, I don't even believe in horoscopes."

Rebbie hovered over her. "Some people are dense," Rebbie said to Lydia as if Jane Ann weren't there at all. "Some people don't appreciate the trouble other people go to. Some people don't even realize I made a special trip out here on Sunday to check where Hugh's house is. Some people don't even know their own fate when they trip over it."

Jane Ann looked at the house and back to Rebbie. "Reb, horoscopes are—"

"Horoscopes are *true*," Rebbie said. "*Pisces, Tuesday, October 22.* That's you. *Well-timed visit to residence of a key person will ensure success in important venture.* I took the trouble to remember your rotten horoscope because I thought you were interested, you crumb!"

"I am, but—"

"Well then. *Important venture* is the play, right? *Key person* is Hugh Turner, the director. *Take partners along.* That's us. *Romance in evening.* Maybe Neil Delancy will call up and say he loves you passionately."

Jane Ann glanced at her bicycle lying on the ground across the road. What she felt like doing was jumping up, grabbing her bike, and escaping. Rebbie and Lydia were only trying to help, but riding seven miles after tryouts, hiding in the bushes like a couple of little kids playing trick-or-treat, taking the chance of coming face to face with Mr. Turner on his front lawn—the whole bit was insane. "Horoscopes are O.K. for laughs," she said, "but I don't believe in them. If I was best at tryouts, I'll get the part."

"You *were* best," Lydia said.

Rebbie squatted close to her. "That's right. You *were* best. But we don't want to take any chances. What if Phyllis the Woodpecker got the part? She didn't do too bad today for such a bird. Want Phyllis to play the part of Emily? Do you?"

"No." Jane Ann remembered the sound of Phyllis's wood-splintering voice. "But why do we have to *see* Mr. Turner? The horoscope doesn't say *See key person*."

"It says a *well-timed visit*," Rebbie repeated. "We've got to be sure he's home. Otherwise it's not well timed."

"Rebbie, his car's in the driveway," Jane Ann said. "He's *home*. Come on—let's go. What do you say, Lyddy?"

"Whatever you want. This is for you."

"Right, it's for you, *Jannie*," Rebbie prodded, giving a sarcastic twist to the nickname that Mr. Turner had started. "Look," she said. "I'll tell you what. You and Lydia keep on hiding here, and I'll go by myself and ring the doorbell. He won't see me. I'll ring and run." Rebbie pushed through a gap in the hedge.

"Reb!" Jane Ann whispered, but Rebbie didn't stop.

Lydia put her fingers to her lips. "Shhh! Let her go."

Jane Ann, crouching low, felt faint, giddy. "I have to go to the bathroom," she said.

Lydia laughed. "Go along with Rebbie then. Say, 'Mr. Turner, I was just passing by and I wondered if I could use your john—' "

"Lydia, shut your mouth!" Jane Ann strained to look over the hedge at the spot where Rebbie stood on the lawn, halfway between them and the porch.

"Should I wait and say 'Hi, Hugh' when he answers?" Rebbie called in a loud whisper.

"No!"

"I'll just say, 'Hugh, Jane Ann Morrow asked

me to tell you she's deeply in love with you, and she'd like the lead in the play.' O.K.?"

"Rebbie!" Jane Ann cried under her breath. The thing was, Rebbie might do or say anything. Nothing embarrassed her. Rebbie was always making flip remarks to teachers. She always acted as if she had nothing to lose. There was never a part she wanted in a play, no high marks she cared about getting, no good reputation to protect.

Rebbie moved across the lawn and up the porch steps. Jane Ann breathed quickly. She thought she heard the doorbell ring. "Rebbie, run!" she whispered, but Rebbie's form still loomed in the doorway.

The door seemed to quiver. Rebbie ducked behind the coach seat.

"Rebbie, run!" Lydia exploded. Half laughing and half crying, Lydia grabbed Jane Ann and they both toppled over. Jane Ann bit the insides of her cheeks to get control of herself as she slowly raised her head. Rebbie was gone. Someone else was standing in the doorway. It was Mr. Turner. Jane Ann wanted to disappear, but she couldn't make herself lie down. Mr. Turner was glancing first to the left and then to the right. He was calling to someone inside. Jane Ann lifted her head higher. *Anything* for a look at Mrs. Turner. Where was Rebbie? Jane Ann searched the bushes for a bulky shadow, but Rebbie wasn't in sight.

Mr. Turner stood by himself at the top of the steps. He seemed to be looking across the lawn now, and Jane Ann flattened her body until she could taste dirt. *Don't see me, Hugh,* she prayed. Next to her, Lydia lay motionless. Jane Ann shifted until she could see Mr. Turner through a space in the hedge. He was searching the sky, taking in the smell of crushed leaves and over-ripe apples. *Let me remember this,* she thought. Then Mr. Turner took one more look around, went inside, and closed the door.

The only sound was dry leaves skittering.

Lydia got up cautiously. "Where's Rebbie?"

"Here I am." Rebbie's foghorn whisper came from behind the apple tree in the side yard. "What a goof!" she called, running toward them. "He didn't see us!"

"But we saw him," Jane Ann said. She helped Rebbie through the hedge. "Move it, Reb. Get your bike. Hurry!" With one eye on the house, Jane Ann picked up her bicycle, turned her headlights on, and took off.

The three bikes rattled along the unpaved road in the direction of the highway. "Shhh!" Jane Ann begged until they were out of sight of the house. Under the street light at the end of the lane Lydia drew up next to her.

"He looked so poetic, Jane Ann, didn't he?" Lydia said softly as they peddled side by side. "He looked so romantic standing there gazing at the moon."

Lydia saw things the same way she did, Jane Ann thought.

"Hey, you two!" Rebbie huffed from behind. "That's crummy, after all I've done—pedaling fast and leaving me. Wait a second!" Catching up, she cut them off and pulled over to the side of the road. "Man, I'm beat," Rebbie said. "Let's walk the bikes up to Route 51."

Even from the dirt lane they could see that traffic on the highway was heavy in both directions. It would be rough bicycling in the dark. Her parents would have a fit if they knew, Jane Ann thought. *So what.* She felt carefree and light-headed. The horoscope seemed to take on new meaning now that she had been to Hugh Turner's house, seen him in person, heard his voice.

"Hey, Reb," she said as the three of them turned onto the gravelly shoulder of the highway, "do you really think that did it? Will I get the part?"

Rebbie nodded, her face rosy in the reflected

lights of a passing car. "You're a Pisces, so naturally you're insecure. You've got to trust in a Leo like me, that's all. We're sure of ourselves. You're getting the part—I feel it in my gut. Hey," Rebbie said, digging her heels into the soft surface next to the highway, "look at this hill, will you? I'll race you both down!"

Jane Ann, edging closer to Rebbie, watched the stream of cars and trucks speeding down the incline and fading away until they were pairs of red eyes in the night. Lydia came up even with them so that they were three abreast.

"It's steep," Jane Ann said. "And look at the traffic!"

"I don't mean there. I mean here on the side— on the shoulder."

"It's bumpy. Come on, no racing."

"O.K.," Rebbie said briskly, "suit yourself." She swung around and pushed off.

"Don't!" Jane Ann called, but Rebbie was gone. Her hair puffed out in the wind. Jane Ann watched her fly.

"Well?" Lydia said.

"Here goes nothing." Jane Ann rolled forward cautiously. Lydia's tires crunched behind her. Her own front wheel sprayed up loose gravel. Cars swished by on the left. A chilly blast of air in her face first surprised her, then gave her new energy. Ahead Rebbie was building up speed. "Too fast!" Jane Ann cried, but the wind blew her words back at her. If Rebbie with her excess pounds could fly, then she could fly too. She could do anything Rebbie could do. She let up on her brakes. Suddenly, swooping down the steepest stretch, she knew she wasn't in control. The bike could either stay with her or shoot out from under. So what! She abandoned herself to the bicycle, the slope of the hill, the rough surface. Her hair blew wildly; a strand of it clung to her lips. Squinting, she watched Rebbie disappear at the bottom. *Slow down*, Jane Ann told herself, but she didn't listen to her own advice until the hill leveled off. Bike brakes screeched, and through eyes full of tears from the wind, she saw Rebbie in the grass by the side of the highway. Next to Rebbie lay her overturned bicycle. Jane Ann squeezed the hand brakes hard and scuffed to a halt.

"Rebbie! Are you hurt?" Jane Ann dropped her bike and ran to the spot where Rebbie lay. "Hey! Are you O.K.?"

"Naturally I'm O.K.," Rebbie whispered, "but pretend to Lydia that I had a fatal accident." She dropped her head back, twisted her face, and stared straight up. An automobile horn blasted as it rushed past them.

"Reb," Jane Ann said, "cut it out! I'm not playing such stupid games. Drivers will think it's real. And we're so damned late. I'll get hung!"

Lydia, panting, skidded to a stop. "What's the matter?"

"Rebbie's being funny."

"What's she doing?" Lydia walked her bike toward them until she could see Rebbie's face. "Oh, my God, Rebbie, please don't do that to your eyes!"

"Come on, Reb!" Jane Ann felt like kicking her. "It's late!"

"All right, crummy sports." Rebbie sat up. Her voice was hoarse. "One question first."

"No!" Lydia groaned. "Not a President question!"

"Not now, Reb. Get your bike."

Rebbie waited as a truck rumbled by, deafening them. "Which President of the United States was shot and died ten weeks later of blood poisoning?" she shouted.

"Lincoln," Lydia said.

"Wrong!"

"James A. Garfield," Jane Ann said. "You asked me that one before, Reb. Now for Pete's sake, move it!"

Rebbie got to her feet slowly and lifted up her bike. She swung one leg over the seat. "Pedaling this thing is a pain in the ass," she said. "Give me a car any day."

"Car!" Jane Ann sniffed. "Won't you ever quit trying to sound cool?"

"Trying? To *sound* cool? I *am* cool."

"You're not old enough for a permit. You can't drive a car."

"Want to bet?"

"So when did you drive?"

"Sunday," she said.

"Whose car?" Lydia asked.

"My brother's. When he was home from school."

"He let you?" Jane Ann looked at her skeptically. "Where'd you go?"

"Out here." Rebbie waved toward the hill. "To Hugh's house. I had to check out where he lives for you, didn't I? I'd do anything for a friend, Jannie old kid. Remember that."

2

"I *said* I was sorry the minute I came in the door!" Jane Ann laid down her fork. The kitchen was quiet except for the boring hum of the refrigerator and the sound of her baby sister, Beth, sucking noisily. Jane Ann watched Beth stick a fist in her mouth and pull it out coated with soggy cookie, while her parents sat there drinking their coffee, not saying a word. A wet, jagged piece of cookie fell to the floor. It was enough to make a person sick. Beth wailed and stretched out her arms to be picked up, but Jane Ann ignored her.

"Just saying you're sorry when you've come in an hour and a half late for dinner doesn't make everything all right." Mrs. Morrow got up from the table and gave Beth another cookie. "When you didn't come at six I fed Beth, but Dad and I waited—we were worried. It's not like you to . . . Hand me those dishes."

Mr. Morrow and Jane Ann passed dishes to her. The harsh clatter of plates, the jangling of silverware, and Beth's sucking noises set Jane Ann on edge.

"I told you I thought I'd be right back." She gave a shrug.

"Right back from Mercer's Hill, ten miles away?"

"Seven," Jane Ann said.

"Seven's bad enough, Jane Ann," Mr. Morrow said. "You know better." Usually when dinner was over her father tipped his chair back in a relaxed way and asked questions about what had happened during the day. But now he was leaning forward, studying the palm of one hand and tapping it with the fingertips of the other. "What were you doing out there, anyway?" he asked patiently, as if he expected her to have a sensible answer.

"Nothing. Just riding." He'd never believe that. Jane Ann hated lying, but she wasn't going to go into details about Mr. Turner and horoscopes. "We got back O.K.," she said, "and I told you I won't do it again, so can't we drop it?"

"Drop it?" Mrs. Morrow's voice was like a knife scraping a plate. "*I* didn't know you were O.K. all the while I was looking out into the dark and telephoning your friends. And speaking of friends, I can't help noticing that any time rules are disregarded in this house Rebbie Hellerman is involved."

"She *is not!*" Jane Ann heard her voice quaver.

Why did that happen whenever she had a disagreement with her parents?

"Rebbie's parents don't seem to make any rules for her," Mrs. Morrow went on, "so naturally she doesn't know there are such things for other people."

"Don't blame Rebbie!" Jane Ann said. She hated losing her cool.

"We're not blaming Rebbie," Mr. Morrow said. "We hold you responsible for your own actions. You were late for dinner, which was inconsiderate. But the main thing is that you were riding a bicycle in the dark on Route 51, and that's dangerous. That's the main point."

Jane Ann made a face. Her father was always coming up with maddening main points that made sense. Her mother usually skipped main points. She preferred to go by tones of voice and facial expressions, to dig up past arguments and to imagine what other people not in the room would say if they were there. Somehow, though, for two such opposite arguers, her parents always ended up siding with each other against her.

"What is that face supposed to mean?" her mother asked.

"If I made a face," Jane Ann said, struggling to keep control, "it's because I already apologized, but you keep going. You act like I do only what other people tell me to—you act like I'm too dumb to make up my own mind!"

"That's not so," said Mrs. Morrow. "You have a lot of common sense. I wish I could say the same for your friend Rebbie."

"Why do you always have to put Rebbie down? Just because her mother—she can't help it that—" Jane Ann felt her eyes filling up. Beth reached out again and Jane Ann took her out of the high chair. Sometimes it wasn't bad having a little sister. Holding Beth on her lap served as protection. It was good to have Beth to hide behind when she didn't want to show her feelings.

Mrs. Morrow closed the door of the dishwasher and sat down. "I don't mean to be hard on Rebbie," she said. "I feel sorry for the girl. She's a pleasant girl, but she's always into something. And what I know about her family doesn't make me feel any better about the time you spend with her. That's another thing. I wish you wouldn't go over there at cocktail time. Before dinner in the evening is when Mrs. Hellerman is in the worst shape, they say."

"They—who's *they?* You don't even know people who are friends of the Hellermans!"

"It's common knowledge, Jane Ann." Mrs. Morrow leaned over to pick up the piece of cookie on the floor. "Mrs. Hellerman's been in and out of hospitals for years. I don't hold that against Rebbie, but I just don't think that house is a good environment."

Jane Ann lifted Beth up so that her own face was buried in Beth's soft middle. Her voice cracked. "Are you telling me not to go to Rebbie's house any more?"

Her mother paused. Jane Ann, shifting Beth, sneaked a look at her parents. The two of them had a way of making a decision by exchanging glances. Nonverbal communication, Mr. Turner called it in English class.

"We believe in guidelines," her father said, "but we don't make that kind of decision for you. *You'll* have to decide whether you're better off staying away from Rebbie and her house." He gave Jane Ann a steady look. "I'm disappointed that you kept us waiting tonight and made us worry. But since you don't make a habit of it, I think a reminder is enough this time. No television or telephone calls this evening, either in or out. It's a light penalty—just a reminder to use that good sense from now on." He squeezed Beth's sticky hand. "Now, if you can get along without me, I'm going to get started on my inventories. The pressure's on," he said to Mrs. Morrow. They exchanged another glance that only the two of them understood, and he left the kitchen.

"Jane Ann . . ." Mrs. Morrow began wiping the table with a sponge. After an argument, her mother always spoke softly. Maybe that was her way of showing she was sorry. "Jane Ann, please put Beth in her pajamas. Jane Ann?"

"What?"

"You understand why I worry, don't you?"

"I guess so." Jane Ann got up and stood without flinching as Beth tugged at her hair.

"Why did you go out riding so late after your tryouts?"

"It was just for . . . luck."

"Riding in the dark—for luck? You were lucky you got home alive."

"I know it sounds crazy, but . . ." For a second she considered telling her mother about Mr. Turner, about going to his house. No, forget it. Her mother would think she was silly—spying on a teacher, believing in astrology.

"Don't you think you'd have better luck coming home and studying the part in the play? How did the tryouts go?"

"Fine," she said, grabbing Beth's wrist. "Stop pulling, Beth! They went fine, but lots of kids are good—Vicky and Suzanne—even Phyllis. I need luck."

"You've always had good luck before, haven't you? Last year you—"

"This year Mr. Turner is directing," she said. "Mr. Turner is practically *professional*." Saying his name brought back the memory of the hedge, the smell of dry leaves and apples, of him standing on the porch.

"When will he tell you?"

"It's going to be posted outside his homeroom at eight thirty tomorrow morning."

"I think you'll be in the play, don't you?"

"I don't just want to be in the play, I want to be Emily."

"Well, let's hope. You've always done well. Miss Brightburn tells Aunt Bea all the time how well you do."

"*Brightburn*—yecch!" Jane Ann squeezed Beth hard. "How can Aunt Bea have a friend like her?"

"Now what's wrong?" Her mother's voice changed to the scraping knife again. "What's wrong with Miss Brightburn?"

"She's nosy."

"Isn't a guidance counselor supposed to be interested in students?"

"She's so phony, so old-fashioned! She wears these yecchy glasses with rhinestones set in the frames. And everything shocks her."

"I'd probably be shocked, too, if I heard the confessions that woman must hear." Mrs. Morrow sponged crumbs into her palm.

"Are you kidding? Nobody tells *her* anything personal." Jane Ann touched her hair and felt a sticky place. "Beth!" she moaned.

"Well, I don't like the way you're always so ready to criticize adults," said Mrs. Morrow. "That's another one of—"

"Stop bugging me!" Jane Ann snapped at Beth. "I'm taking Beth up," she said. *Sorry I was late,* she had meant to say again, but she didn't say it.

Upstairs in Beth's room Jane Ann hoisted her up on a chair and began to take off her stretch suit. Ugh. She hated arguments, would almost rather surrender than say mean things she'd be sorry for later. Every time a disagreement with her parents ended, she swore it wouldn't happen again. Next time she'd be so calm, so mature. She would stop it before it started.

"Ba-mas," Beth said as Jane Ann slipped on her pajama top.

This time, of course, she had brought on the whole thing by being late. She'd been willing to take her medicine. It had been worth it. The thing that had really gotten to her, though, was her

mother's dragging Rebbie in, talking as if Jane
Ann were some robot that Rebbie wound up.

A safety pin popped open. "Lie still!" she
shouted at Beth. No wonder Rebbie was the way
she was, Jane Ann thought. People were always
down on her. Teachers got on her back because
they said she never did any work except memorizing dumb facts about Presidents. Parents didn't
like Rebbie because they heard she smoked and
broke rules—like the business of driving the car.
Or they thought she was freaked out for believing
in astrology. Even a lot of *kids* gave Rebbie a
hard time, mocking her because she was overweight, kidding around that her father was a
crooked lawyer, turning Rebecca H. Hellerman
into nicknames like "Rebbie the Rebel" or "Rebbie
H. Hellion." Brightburn was always threatening
to do a psychological workup on Rebbie, whatever
that was.

Jane Ann fiddled at the snaps on Beth's pajamas. "Hold still, Bethie," she said, forcing herself
to be patient. Only a couple of people, she
thought—mostly herself and Lydia—really appre-
ciated Rebbie. Since that day in fourth grade
when Rebbie had first gotten to be her good
friend, Jane Ann had spent a lot of time trying to
figure her out, so that by now she was a sort of
Rebbie expert. First, Rebbie was never phony. If
she didn't like something, she told you right out.
That made a lot of adults afraid of her. Second, if
she liked you, she was extremely loyal. And third,
she was really clever. Some people thought her
sense of humor was weird—*sick* even. For instance, some people would probably think it was
too much that Rebbie had sent Brightburn an
anonymous copy of *A Playgirl's Guide to Sex* in a
plain wrapper—to her school address. But Jane
Ann admired the way Rebbie's mind took big
original jumps instead of plodding along in the
same old way.

On the other hand, Rebbie could be aggravating

sometimes—too big a show-off, too disrespectful. But the good definitely outweighed the bad. Who was measuring, anyway? Some people you were drawn to whether it was sensible or not. Well, at least Rebbie had her and Lydia. And there was one teacher she got along with—Mr. Turner.

Jane Ann fastened the last snap and patted Beth's bottom. "Up you go!" she said. *Mr. Turner.* She pictured him gazing at the moon. She stood Beth up on the chair and pretended that Beth was Mr. Turner.

"Thank you for choosing me to play Emily," she whispered. Beth laughed. "I didn't really expect to get the part," Jane Ann said. No, that was a lie. There was a good chance that her name would be posted. Vicky Lindstrom might get it, though, Jane Ann thought. Vicky looked right, and she had read the lines pretty well. Suzanne Garrett was a better actress than Vicky, but she had been nervous. Lydia would be perfect for the role of Emily—delicate and sensitive—and she could act, too, but Lydia hadn't even tried out for *Our Town.* Lydia was going to take art lessons. Anything, _anything_—just so Phyllis Cooper didn't get the part.

"Phyllis *is* animated," Jane Ann admitted to the imaginary Mr. Turner, "but she's not really a natural actress." Beth gurgled and jumped up and down. How horrible if the role went to Phyllis the Woodpecker. Jane Ann and Rebbie had once overheard Miss Brightburn telling a teacher, "Phyllis Cooper is so marvelously *animated!*" "She's animated all right," Rebbie had said afterward, "just like Woody Woodpecker." The only thing Phyllis had going for her, as far as Jane Ann could see, was her wood-splintering voice. One thing about Phyllis—you could hear her in the last row.

"Phyllis doesn't really look the part. Do you think I look the part, Hugh?" she said to Beth. Beth grabbed Jane Ann's hands. In Jane Ann's opinion her own face was O.K.—not as delicate as Lydia's, but O.K.

"I'm just the right height," she told Beth, "especially if Neil Delancy plays the part of George Gibbs. Oh, Mr. Turner . . ." she said, "oh . . . Hugh . . .?" Jane Ann put her hands on Beth's waist. "Hugh . . . getting this part is the most important venture of my life, and you're the key person. Hugh . . . will I get it?" she whispered. Beth stretched out her arms, and Jane Ann, lifting her off the chair, gave her a hug. "You don't know how much this means to me, Hugh," she said.

"Time to go to bed now, Beth," Jane Ann leaned against the raised side of the crib and lowered Beth into it. "Mommy'll be up in a minute."

"Mommy!" Beth whimpered.

"Be nice, Bethie. Here's Fuzzball." Jane Ann handed her the ball of fur with a tiny snout that was Beth's favorite toy. "Good night, Beth. Good night, Fuzzball!" Jane Ann tiptoed out.

Privacy at last. She loved being alone in the room that had been hers since she was born. With the door shut she could forget everything outside and concentrate on reading *Our Town*, writing poems, and putting things in her diary. The room wasn't large like Rebbie's or Lydia's, but it had everything she needed—an old rolltop desk with lots of pigeonholes, a counter for projects that called for space, and the old bed with a design handpainted by her grandfather who had died when she was little. Almost everything in the room reminded her of people and places she loved. And the window looked out onto an ever-changing scene in the backyard—forsythia and peonies in spring, tomatoes and hollyhocks in summer, and all year round the playhouse surrounded by big round boxwood trees. She had grown up in that yard, an only child until age thirteen. Then at thirteen—it had embarrassed her when her parents had first broken the news—Beth had been born, proving that you could never sit back and count on things staying the way they were.

Jane Ann took her algebra book out of her bicycle bag and spread it open on the desk top. The telephone rang. No telephone calls for her the whole evening, she remembered. *Romance in evening,* her horoscope had promised. But even if that was Neil Delancy on the phone right now, she wouldn't be allowed to speak to him.

The telephone stopped ringing. She heard footsteps coming upstairs. It must be her mother going into Beth's room. It couldn't have been Neil on the phone. Neil had never called her before. Why would he call now? Anyway, Neil was too shy to telephone a girl. The horoscope was a fake. She wasn't going to have any *romance in evening.*

Suddenly, as she heard her mother go downstairs, Jane Ann started to feel peculiar, lightheaded. She knew the feeling. She even had a name for it—the Scary Feeling. The Scary Feeling was the wave of panic that came over her sometimes. It had started when she was nine or ten years old. It came on her when she was alone, and usually it only stayed a few minutes. But during those few minutes she had the sensation of being separated from everything and everybody, as if she were alone on a planet and couldn't remember who she was. *I know who I am!* she told herself as the Scary Feeling swooped down, but still she was afraid to try to say her name or where she lived. What if she couldn't remember?

It's silly, she told herself. I *like* being by myself! It'll go away in a minute. But meanwhile her palms sweated and she gulped hard. *I'm me,* she thought. *I know who I am.* And then to prove to herself that the Scary Feeling was nonsense, she put her head down on the desk and forced herself to recite silently, as if some judge were listening: "I'm Jane Ann Morrow. I live at 814 Oak Street, Windsor, Pennsylvania. My parents are James and Evelyn Morrow. My sister is Beth Morrow.

My friends are Rebbie Hellerman and Lydia Haverd. I'm in ninth grade at Windsor Junior High School. Tomorrow I'll find out if I got the part of Emily in *Our Town,* a play by Thornton Wilder directed by Mr. Hugh Turner." When she could say it all, not once but twice, she felt a little better. She took a deep breath and prepared to start her algebra. There was a knock at the door.

Her mother opened it a crack. "You had a phone call from Lydia," she said. "She'll speak to you tomorrow in school about going with her to her art lesson."

Her mother's voice chased away the last remnant of the Scary Feeling, and when she was alone again, Jane Ann felt perfectly normal. Did other people get the Scary Feeling, she wondered. She was almost glad to turn to her algebra—to an assignment that was fixed and definite and took her mind off herself. When she had finished, Jane Ann unlocked the drawer, took out her notebook, and wrote a few lines of poetry without being sure whether they were to Neil or to Mr. Turner.

"Good night, I'm going to sleep," she called down to her parents.

"Good night!" her mother said.

She heard her father coming up the stairs. "Good night," he said from the doorway. "I hope you get the part you want in the play. Good luck."

"Thanks." The battle was officially over. That was one thing she had to say for her parents— they tried not to hold grudges. "I won't be late again," she whispered, hoping she could stick to it.

When her father had gone down again she felt very tired, but sleep was long in coming; and when she dozed off, she dreamed. In one of her dreams Miss Brightburn was knocking on Rebbie's door—except that it was the door to the playhouse in the boxwood trees. "I'm here to do a psychological workup!" Brightburn was calling to

Rebbie. Brightburn was wearing her famous
rhinestone glasses. "Go fly a kite!" Rebbie said,
thumbing her nose at Miss Brightburn. And because it was a dream, Brightburn did.

3

"Did you hear anything yet, Jane Ann?" Phyllis
Cooper stuck her head inside the homeroom.

"No," Jane Ann said. Phyllis knew the names
were going up at eight thirty—she was just playing dumb. Now she was heading toward her, looking like a fashion model as usual. You had to hand
it to Phyllis—she had great clothes. She was one
of those kids who knew how to put outfits together without having to buy things off a rack
marked "Coordinates."

Phyllis leaned over close to Jane Ann. "You're
going to get the part!" she said in an exaggerated
whisper. Probably Phyllis expected her to say,
"Oh, no, *you* will."

"We'll find out at eight thirty," Jane Ann said.

"Got to go!" Phyllis touched Jane Ann's arm
apologetically. Phyllis turned friendliness on and
off as if it came out of a faucet. "Got to see *somebody* before the late bell rings." Some boy probably, or maybe Mr. Turner. "Oh, hi!" Jane Ann
heard Phyllis's voice in the hall. Ugh, she
thought—*animated*. "Hi, Miss Brightburn!"
Phyllis was saying.

Brightburn? Straight out of her dream. Jane
Ann smiled: Brightburn knocking on the door of
the playhouse; Rebbie thumbing her nose; Brightburn flying a kite.

Miss Brightburn appeared in the doorway. "Is Mrs. Nolan here? Oh, Jane Ann," she said, "you're the one I'm looking for."

"Me?" It was weird to have a person out of your dream come looking for you. It was like a horoscope coming true.

"Yes, *you*, dear." Miss Brightburn handed her a pink slip of paper. "As soon as the eight fifteen bell rings, I'd like to see you in my office."

"This morning?"

"Yes, during homeroom period. I have to see someone else now, but when Mrs. Nolan comes in, give her the pink slip and come to me at eight fifteen."

"I have to—will I—?" *Will I be finished in time to check the list for the play?* she was about to ask, but Miss Brightburn interrupted.

"And, Jane Ann, tell Mrs. Nolan that Rebbie Hellerman won't be in today. She has an emergency. I'll see you in a few minutes then."

An emergency? Jane Ann wanted to find out more, but Miss Brightburn was gone. What could be wrong with Rebbie? She'd been perfectly O.K. at seven thirty last night. Rebbie would have telephoned, unless—maybe Rebbie had called and her mother had forgotten to tell her or had purposely kept it from her.

Jane Ann fidgeted. "Lyddy!" she called with relief.

Lydia, carrying her big, black art portfolio, came toward Jane Ann's desk. "Your parents were mad last night, weren't they?" Lydia set down the portfolio and a newspaper.

"Yeah, but they cooled off finally. Hey, did you hear anything from Rebbie?"

"No, why?"

"Brightburn just told me Reb had an emergency. I'm supposed to see Brightburn when the bell rings. It must be about Rebbie."

"Emergency? Oh, God, with her it could be anything. Maybe Brightburn got the sex book Rebbie sent her, and she suspects!"

"Shhh! Nobody's supposed to know about that but us."

"If that's what it is, don't rat on her."

"Are you kidding? I wouldn't."

"Jane Ann, the tryouts—the list. Meet me the second she lets you go. At Hugh Turner's homeroom. And look," Lydia said, holding out a newspaper, "I brought this to show you—your horoscope for today."

Jane Ann took it. Out of the corner of her eye she saw Mrs. Nolan come into the room. *Morning favorable for news,* the horoscope said. *Don't let a bigwig knuckle you under. Keep aspirations high in evening.*

"Favorable for news." Lydia smiled. "News about the play, I hope."

Jane Ann curled the corner of the paper. "I'm nervous, Lyddy. Thanks for bringing me this. I hope it's right." The bell rang.

Lydia grabbed her arm. "I'll go to Hugh's room as fast as I can when homeroom's over and look at the cast list," she said.

"O.K. Oh, wait a second. Lyddy, let me look up Rebbie's sign for today." Jane Ann scanned the paper for LEO (JULY 22 TO AUGUST 21). *Cater to family affairs in* A.M. *In* P.M. *try to find congenial companions. Be daring.* "Well," Jane Ann handed the newspaper back to Lydia, "at least it doesn't say anything terrible. I'm going to Brightburn now. I'll see you."

"Jane Ann, I almost forgot. Will you come with me to Greenmore after school? My dad's going to fix it up for me to take art lessons."

"If we don't go by bicycle and if you promise we won't get back late."

"No bicycles! We'll be back before six. Maybe your mother'll let you stay to supper."

"I'll go with you—unless Rebbie needs us."

"Naturally, if Rebbie needs us—"

"See you by Mr. Turner's room."

"Jane Ann—good luck!"

Jane Ann handed the pink slip to Mrs. Nolan and walked into the quiet hall. She always felt nervous about going to the guidance office. Some kids had guidance counselors they were close to. Some kids told their counselors about personal problems, but Jane Ann couldn't imagine telling Brightburn "I'm unhappy because Neil Delancy doesn't call me up" or "I want the part in the play so much!" or "I get this Scary Feeling sometimes." And she'd *never* tell that Rebbie had sent the sex book.

She passed the auditorium and knocked on the door of Miss Brightburn's office, a compartment that was the guidance department's idea of privacy. Anything that was said could float over the partitions. Eavesdropping for one period, Jane Ann figured, you could probably get enough stuff to blackmail half the school.

"Jane Ann, come in!" Brightburn was at her desk flipping through a stack of permanent record cards with photographs attached that made everyone look like a juvenile delinquent. "Put your books down and take a seat," she said. "I'll be with you in a minute."

Please hurry, Jane Ann thought. She looked around to see if there was any sign of the sex book. There sure were enough hiding places for it, with all the drawers and filing cabinets. Jane Ann sat and stared at the mug shots on the backs of the record cards. She wondered if Miss Brightburn would let her see her own record if she asked. What was on it would be good stuff, she knew. Teachers liked her because she was polite and always pretended to be interested even if she wasn't. She never bugged them the way Rebbie did. *Oh, for Pete's sake,* she thought, *hurry up!*

"There!" Miss Brightburn laid down the record cards. "Now. How's your Aunt Bea?"

"Fine."

"Good." She smiled. "I suppose you wonder why I called you in—a good student like you with no academic problems?"

"Does it have something to do with Rebbie Hellerman?" Jane Ann asked.

"Yes, it does!"

"What happened?" The muscles tightened in Jane Ann's stomach.

"Happened? Nothing's happened to Rebbie. She's out of school today because her mother was taken to the hospital, but that's only an indirect reason why I called you in." Miss Brightburn smiled again.

Jane Ann sighed. That made sense. Mrs. Hellerman was in the hospital. *The woman's been in and out of hospitals for years,* Jane Ann's own mother had said just last night.

"What's wrong with Mrs. Hellerman?" she asked.

Miss Brightburn gave her a peculiar look. Or maybe it was just that the sun was reflecting off her rhinestone-studded glasses. "Mrs. Hellerman's in the *county* hospital," she said. By the way she said *county* Jane Ann realized that she meant the part of it that was for mental patients. *In and out of hospitals*—Mrs. Hellerman drank a lot, but she wasn't crazy—was she?

"But I understand she's not staying there," Miss Brightburn went on. "Rebbie's father's on his way back from a business trip and has arranged for Mrs. Hellerman to come home tomorrow. Jane Ann," Miss Brightburn's face changed expression. "Jane Ann, the reason I called you in is that . . . I'm worried."

Jane Ann nodded. She was worried too. She had realized something was wrong with Mrs. Hellerman, but she hadn't known how bad it was.

"I've been meaning for some time to speak to you," Miss Brightburn said, "but the call from the hospital this morning reminded me of the urgency of this. Jane Ann, I've noticed, and your teachers bear me out on this, that you spend a good deal of time with Rebbie Hellerman. Is that right?"

"Yes," Jane Ann answered slowly.

"Then I'm sure it hasn't escaped you—especially after this unpleasantness we've been discussing just now—that you're involved with a girl who has serious problems that affect her behavior and schoolwork."

"Yes," Jane Ann said.

"Do you realize the danger of this?" Miss Brightburn slowly tapped a warning on the desk top with her pen point.

"Yes," Jane Ann whispered. So *that* was all Miss Brightburn had called her in for—to tell her Rebbie might flunk—try to help her, be her friend, be a good influence on her. Teachers had often suggested that before.

"Good!" Miss Brightburn seemed relieved. "I'm glad you understand the danger to you in a relationship with Rebbie Hellerman." She spoke in a low voice, as if she expected the eavesdroppers to be straining their ears in the next compartment.

"Danger to *me*?" Jane Ann repeated stupidly.

Miss Brightburn's eyes seemed to be magnified behind her glasses. "Yes, danger to _you_. I wouldn't talk this way about the Hellermans to just any student, Jane Ann, but as a friend of your aunt, I think I'm entitled to give you a little extra bit of advice." Miss Brightburn leaned forward, "My advice, Jane Ann, is to drop Rebbie."

"Drop her?" Jane Ann sat up straight. "You mean . . . ?" She wasn't sure she had heard right.

"Yes," Miss Brightburn nodded, narrowing her eyes, "find a way to ease out of your relationship. I would if I were you."

"But she's my friend!" Jane Ann said. Suddenly a picture rose up before her of Rebbie leading the way, flying down Mercer's Hill on her bicycle, playing dead. "Rebbie's not a bad person—we have a lot of fun together."

"I'm sure you think so," Miss Brightburn

agreed. "And believe me, I know your intentions are good. You think you can help Rebbie. But Jane Ann, you're too good-hearted. You can't help her, dear. Rebbie needs professional help, and we're doing our best to try to get her to accept it. Drop Rebbie, Jane Ann, and stick with your nicer friends. Healthier relationships will be even more fun."

Jane Ann felt herself turning hot. "Rebbie's been my friend since fourth grade!"

"I realize that," Miss Brightburn said. "But do you keep a friend you've outgrown just for old times' sake? Rebbie's a child who's very, very mixed up. Jane Ann, believe me, Rebbie would like nothing better than to take advantage of an inexperienced girl like you. That's why I called *you* in and not the one or two others who are friends with Rebbie. Lydia Haverd, for instance, seems to be less easily influenced."

"But . . ." Jane Ann wished she could strike out, punch Miss Brightburn. That's probably what Rebbie would do. Instead tears welled up in her eyes so that she was afraid to move her head. Which was worse, the nerve of Brightburn telling her who to be friends with, or the insult about how dumb and inexperienced she was? "I *like* Rebbie," she said more timidly than she meant to.

"I know," Miss Brightburn said patiently. "But I also know the kind of family you come from, Jane Ann, and I doubt that your parents approve of this relationship with a girl who's rude, who lies, and who hangs out smoking heaven-knows-what in unsavory places."

"Rebbie doesn't lie to me." Jane Ann prayed for the tears not to spill over.

Miss Brightburn shook her head. "The point is, Jane Ann, don't get pulled down by those whose reach isn't as high as yours. Think about my advice. If you do, I'm sure you'll come to agree with me. For your own good, Jane Ann, seek the best, the very *best* in life."

The bell signaling the end of homeroom made Jane Ann jump.

"I'm not going to keep you any longer, dear," said Miss Brightburn, getting up from the desk.

Jane Ann rose quickly and gathered up her books. Seek *what* best, she wondered—friendship with a cartoon character like Phyllis Cooper? She felt as if she ought to say something more, but she didn't know what. "Thanks," she nodded curtly without looking at Miss Brightburn.

"You're welcome, Jane Ann." Miss Brightburn walked her to the door. "Think about what I've said now, and give my best to Aunt Bea! Tell her I'll be speaking to her soon."

Jane Ann burst into the hall. Her eyes burned from holding back tears, her throat felt parched. Why hadn't she fought back? Why did she always go weak in tough situations with adults? Maybe Brightburn was right that she was easily led. Jane Ann stopped at the water fountain and took a long drink. Were Brightburn and her mother both right—that Rebbie was going to lead her into trouble? Rebbie could be a pain sometimes. And, of course, the stuff Brightburn had said about the Hellerman family was true. Jane Ann had never seen so many liquor bottles in one place as in the Hellermans' garbage.

But Rebbie was her *friend*. Drop Rebbie? That was crazy. Not even her mother had suggested that. Jane Ann dabbed water from the fountain onto her forehead. She'd show Brightburn who was easily led and who wasn't. She'd never drop Rebbie. *Tell Aunt Bea I'll be speaking to her soon!* Brightburn had said. So what—let Brightburn call all the Morrow relatives. *Ease out of your relationship.* Jane Ann glowered. She hated Brightburn. Who would drop a good friend? Nobody, she thought—except maybe Phyllis the Woodpecker.

Phyllis—good God—the *play*. Brightburn had shaken her up so much she'd forgotten for fifteen whole minutes about the list. Jane Ann ran down

the hall, her stomach flipping over faster and
faster the closer she got. Even from a distance she
could see the crowd around the bulletin board, and
in the crowd she spotted Lydia. When Lydia saw
her, she gave a little leap and came running.

"You got it, Jane Ann!" she said, hugging her.
"The horoscope was right. You got the lead—
you're Emily!"

4

The bus sped away from the school along Windsor
Boulevard past big homes with wide lawns. Lydia
and Jane Ann, up front behind the driver, sat
back and looked out the window. Windsor was
beautiful in the fall, Jane Ann thought. Oaks and
maples made a red and gold canopy over the boulevard mall. She waited for the bus to turn onto
Greenmore Avenue so that she could be sure to see
the library, a comfortable granite monster with a
duck pond in front.

It was fun sitting next to Lydia, heading for an
appointment at Greenmore College, pretending to
be older. Lydia looked older. People who didn't
know her thought she was sixteen. That was because she wore her hair pulled back, the way her
mother did, and because she acted calm and mature.

The bus stopped at the library and a cluster of
people boarded. Lydia pushed her art portfolio
farther under the seat. "Do you believe in horoscopes now?" she asked when the bus started
again.

"I don't know," Jane Ann said. "Everything

sure worked out. My feet haven't touched the ground the whole day. We have our first rehearsal tomorrow." She held her copy of the playbook close to her.

"I'm glad you and Neil both got leads. Everybody was glad—except Phyllis. Was your mother happy?"

"Yeah. She must've been in a really good mood to let me come and have supper at your house. But then she always says yes when you invite me. She likes you."

"Naturally," Lydia laughed. "I'm a lovable kid. Hey, you know, if your horoscope had just said *Morning favorable for news,* it wouldn't be so unusual, but that *Don't let a bigwig knuckle you under,* that's strange! I still don't understand what Brightburn wanted from you."

"I told you, she wants me to drop Rebbie because she's a bad influence."

"That's ridiculous. That's dumb. Do you think Brightburn got the sex book and guessed that Rebbie sent it?"

"I don't think so. She said she's been meaning to speak to me for a while."

"Why do you think Brightburn spoke only to you?" Lydia asked. "I'm friends with Rebbie too."

"She thinks you can take of yourself. She thinks I'm inexperienced." Jane Ann remembered Miss Brightburn's glittering eyes.

"Did you tell her your friends are none of her business?"

"Sure." Jane Ann looked away quickly. In a way Miss Brightburn *had* knuckled her under. The talk had ended with her *thanking* Brightburn!

"Well, the whole thing's strange," Lydia said. "When I called the hospital at lunchtime they wouldn't tell me anything about Rebbie or her mother. I called the Hellermans' house, and nobody answered—not even the maid. Then I called Mummy. She was working at home this morning, and she said no one phoned. So where do you think Rebbie is?"

"If her horoscope is right, she's looking for congenial companions. Let's just keep trying to call her house. She's got to go there sometime." The bus jerked forward and stopped in heavy traffic. "Lyddy," Jane Ann said in a low voice. "Do you know what's wrong with Mrs. Hellerman?"

"Not really." The bus started again. "I guess she's an alcoholic, but Mummy says—you know my mother works with people who have problems like that—she says drinking too much is usually a sign that other things are wrong. I've never seen Mrs. Hellerman act crazy. Whenever we've seen her she just twitches her mouth a lot and asks to be excused, doesn't she?"

Jane Ann nodded. "Does your mother know Mrs. Hellerman?"

"She used to. They used to know each other a long time ago. Mummy won't talk to me about her because she says it would be unprofessional. But I know Mrs. Hellerman started in like this when Rebbie was little. Mummy likes Rebbie a lot. She's glad I'm friends with her."

Mummy. Jane Ann smiled. It always struck her funny that the whole Haverd family called Mrs. Haverd "Mummy."

"You're lucky," Jane Ann said. "Your mother's great. I wish my mother had a job and was interested in alcoholism and politics and stuff. I mean, my mother's great too, but it must be boring just staying home and taking care of Beth."

"Beth's so cute. Do you think your mother minds?"

"No, she likes it."

"Well then, what do you care, so long as she's happy?"

"Yeah, I guess so. Hey, let's phone Rebbie as soon as we get there," Jane Ann said. She looked out the window again as the bus strained to the top of the steep hill. She saw students riding bicycles and walking along the paths beneath the trees on the campus. And on either side of the street were moss-covered buildings with gold plaques announcing their names—Hapsworth, Wilkinson, Arnold. They were at Greenmore College.

"We'll go to my father's office first," Lydia said. She picked up her portfolio as the bus reached the corner. "He'll show us where to find Daniel Carlino's studio, and then after I see about lessons, Mummy will pick us up on her way home from work."

The bus stopped and they got off. Curled leaves made a crackling sound under their feet as they walked across the gravel path to College Hall. At the entrance they climbed a flight of worn steps and entered a dark corridor. Outside one of the classrooms a few students were talking to a professor, but the rest of College Hall was silent. Lydia led Jane Ann up another set of stairs to a door that was partly open. She knocked.

"Yes, come in," said a voice. "Oh, Lyddy, it's you!" Dr. Haverd, working alone at his desk, pushed back his chair and got up. "Hello, Jane Ann, good to see you."

Dr. Haverd, with his beard and tweed jacket, looked the way a professor was supposed to, Jane Ann thought, except that he no longer smoked a pipe. "The Surgeon General convinced me to throw it away," he had told her once. That's how the Haverds were—always studying and looking things up in *Consumer Reports* and the *New York Times Index,* and then doing what was supposed to be the wisest thing.

"How would you like a cup of tea, girls?" he said. "Dan Carlino's tied up in class now. I'll send you there in a few minutes."

"Daddy, I have to make a call to Rebbie," Lydia said. "Her mother's in the hospital. May I use the phone?"

"That's too bad," he said. "Go ahead. Dial six for an outside line. Meanwhile, I'll do the tea hon-

ors. Have a seat, Jane Ann." Dr. Haverd went to
the hot plate and poured boiling water into three
cups.

Jane Ann let her eyes wander around the office. It was cluttered and comfortable, just like
the Haverds' big house. Over Dr. Haverd's desk
was a photograph of Lydia, her mother, her married sister, and her two older brothers. With all
those older kids, Dr. Haverd must be pretty old
himself, Jane Ann guessed, but he was really in
good shape. Maybe she ought to start reading
Consumer Reports and eating organically grown
foods like the Haverds did.

"No answer," Lydia said, holding the receiver
away from her ear.

"Let it ring some more," said Jane Ann. It
would be perfect, Jane Ann imagined as she
watched Dr. Haverd fixing the tea, to have a father who was a professor of literature, a father
who sat around talking about books and plays all
the time. Not that she'd exchange her own father,
of course. Her own father was really nice and had
a good sense of humor when he wasn't talking
about family rules and guidelines, but it wasn't
too exciting to hear him talk about his work—
selling plumbing equipment. Lydia's really lucky,
Jane Ann was thinking, but then she remembered
that Lydia wished her father were an artist. The
way things were in this cockeyed world, probably
there was a poor kid somewhere wishing for a father who sold plumbing equipment.

"No answer," Lydia repeated. She hung up the
receiver and sat down as her father brought the
tea.

"Now, what can you two tell me that's new?" he
asked, fanning his cup.

"Jane Ann got the lead in *Our Town*," Lydia
said.

"Excellent casting! Congratulations!" Dr. Haverd said. "What scene do you like best?"

Jane Ann thought for a moment. "I guess the

scene where Emily comes back from the dead to relive one day of her life. Where she tells her mother to really look at her."

"Good choice," Dr. Haverd said. "Parents and children don't look at each other enough, and I only wish I had more time to look at both of you now." He smiled at Lydia. "And now, Lyddy, my dear, I'll set you in the direction of Duff Hall. Dan's class should be over. Lyddy, I have an article to finish. Mummy's picking you up on her way home, right? I'll see you at home then." Lydia took her portfolio, and Dr. Haverd pointed out the modern building farther along the gravel path. "That's Duff Hall," he said. "See the skylight? That's the studio. You see if Dan'll take you on, Lyddy, and I'll talk to him tomorrow about financial arrangements."

Jane Ann studied the structure of plate glass, satiny metal, and dark wood as they approached the entrance. Duff Hall looked like a space station, she thought—a friendly space station though, not cold and sterile.

"Did you ever meet Daniel Carlino before?" she asked Lydia.

"Yes. He's very good-looking and a good artist."

"Will you call him 'Daniel' if he lets you take lessons from him?"

"Probably," Lydia said. "Artists don't usually get hung up like other people about things like that."

"You're so talented, Lyddy," Jane Ann said.

"I hope Daniel thinks so. He doesn't take just anyone as a pupil."

For a second Jane Ann felt envious. Lydia *was* lucky. Not only was she pretty and mature-looking and talented with great parents who understood her, but she was also poised and natural. What other person their age could say "Daniel" like that without sounding like a fool? Who else could say "he doesn't take just anyone" without

sounding like a snob? Brightburn was right in one
thing at least: Lydia *was* experienced. Lydia
wouldn't come close to bursting into tears in front
of Brightburn. Did you have to be born into a
family like the Haverds to be like Lydia, or could
anyone learn?

Lydia opened the heavy double doors of Duff
Hall. They paused, breathing in a special kind of
rich air that Jane Ann connected with libraries
and museums. In the middle of the lobby was a
metal sculpture.

"Isn't it beautiful?" Lydia whispered. "This is
the way," she said. Their footsteps echoed in the
hall. Lydia stopped outside the studio and peered
through a small window in the door. "They haven't
finished," she said. "They're still working."

"What shall we do?" Jane Ann stood on tiptoe
and saw the students at their drawing boards.

"Let's go in. I love to watch them working." Lydia opened the door.

The studio was full of light. Lydia and Jane
Ann stood tentatively in the doorway. The students continued working; no one looked up. Lydia
trembled. "I love this," she said softly.

A man with dark curly hair waved to them
from across the studio. "That's Daniel," Lydia
whispered.

Jane Ann agreed with Lydia—he was very
handsome. His features looked as if an artist had
sculpted them. Jane Ann felt Lydia touching her
arm lightly. Then Lydia's grip tightened. Jane
Ann glanced in the same direction as Lydia and
drew in her breath. On a platform in front of the
students was a male model. Jane Ann looked long
and steadily at the nude model before she realized
she was staring.

She moved closer to Lydia, but Daniel Carlino
had come over, and he was whispering something
to Lydia. Then Lydia was sitting down at an
empty desk and taking a sketchbook and pencil
out of her portfolio.

Jane Ann shifted uneasily. Should she sit down? There was no other empty seat except up front, close to the model. She rocked back and forth trying to decide whether to go or to stay. One of the boys at the drawing board gave her a peculiar sideways look. Jane Ann tried to be matter-of-fact, but searching around the room for a safe place to fix her eyes, she kept returning to the model, whose golden skin gleamed. His body was smooth, Jane Ann noticed, slim like a runner's. Of course she had seen diagrams of the human body in textbooks and even pictures in books like *A Playgirl's Guide to Sex,* but she had no brothers like Lydia and Rebbie did. This was the very first time she had ever . . . All of a sudden the model shifted slightly so that he was facing her full front.

Jane Ann dropped her eyes and, trying to look occupied, flipped frantically through her playbook. Would it be better to escape, to wait outside, or would that attract even more attention? She could imagine the expression of the student who was watching her if she were to trip going out the door. Her feet were numb, and she felt her face grow hot. Was it because she wasn't an artist, she wondered, that she felt so uncomfortable, felt as if the model might glance up at any second to point to her and shout, "Make her stop looking!" Or was this just another example of being inexperienced?

She *hated* being inexperienced. Lydia didn't quiver when she was called in by a guidance counselor. When Lydia wandered into a studio where a model had no clothes on, she didn't stand on one leg like a crane and turn pink like a flamingo. She pulled out her sketchbook! Rebbie could handle a scene like this. She'd make a joke. It was terrible to be a person who didn't know what to do. On stage, pretending to be someone else, she could look like she was doing the right thing, but how

come, in everyday living, she was so often unsure
of herself?

Through the little window in the door Jane Ann
suddenly saw a familiar face. Mrs. Haverd was
motioning to her to step outside. Thank heaven
for Mrs. Haverd. Jane Ann turned the knob and
closed the door quickly behind her.

"Jane Ann—good! I'm glad I found you. Is Lydia almost finished?" Mrs. Haverd, a taller version of Lydia, leaned over to look through the
window. Something about Mrs. Haverd's appear-
ance—her height and slimness, her neat, casual
clothes, the confidence of her smile—always made
Jane Ann sure that when she was around everything was under control.

"Lydia's sketching," Jane Ann said. She
watched Mrs. Haverd's face.

Mrs. Haverd caught Lydia's eye and waved.
"What is she sketching?"

"A model."

"A life class? Marvelous!" Mrs. Haverd smiled
through the window at Lydia. "What a marvelous
opportunity!"

What would her own mother think, Jane Ann
wondered, if she found her in a roomful of artists
drawing nudes from life? Mrs. Haverd didn't
think anything, except that it was a good thing to
learn. No wonder Lydia was so much more experienced, with a mother like that.

The door opened and Lydia stuck out her head.
"Come in a second, Mummy," she said. "Daniel
wants to speak to you. He'll take me as a student!
You come, too, Jane Ann—come back in!"

"No," Jane Ann shook her head. "Congratulations, Lyddy, but I'll wait in the lobby. I—I want
to look at the sculpture."

"O.K., we'll be just a minute. Jane Ann," Lydia
whispered, "he's going to give me lessons!" The
door swung shut between them.

Jane Ann walked slowly through the deserted
corridor. The model was still in her mind. She pic-

tured him—with Neil's face. Feeling dizzy, she
stopped and leaned against the wall. From there
she caught a full view of the metal sculpture in
the lobby. How did anybody build such a huge
thing in one piece, she wondered. Then she saw
what she hadn't noticed before, that the sculpture
was a male nude. How could you keep calm
enough to get any work done around this place?
Male nudes were everywhere. She came nearer.
Close up, she saw that it wasn't one piece. The to-
tal effect came from the welding together of
thousands of silver filaments. She put out her
hand and rested it on the thigh of the figure.

Voices echoed in the corridor. Jane Ann pulled
her hand back quickly as the students from the
life class passed by. In their bulky sweaters, with
their backs to her, she couldn't pick out the student who had given her the look. Maybe even the
model had walked right by her, she thought—safe
and ordinary in his jeans and sweater.

"Jane Ann!" Lydia handed the portfolio to her
mother and ran to the sculpture. "Jane Ann, he's
so nice! He says I show promise!"

"I knew he would." Jane Ann smiled. She patted the foot of the figure. "Lyddy, look how complicated this is."

Mrs. Haverd caught up with them. "He's very
beautiful," she said. For a minute the three of
them examined the work in silence. "Oh, before I
forget it," Mrs. Haverd said, rummaging in her
handbag, "Rebbie's been trying to reach you two."
She took out a folded piece of paper. "She came
over just before I left the house. I tried to get her
to talk to me, but she preferred to write a note,
and I said I'd bring it along."

Lydia unfolded the note and smoothed it out.
Jane Ann looked over her shoulder.

"It's from Rebbie, all right," Lydia said. "Look
at this."

5

Dear Jannie & Lyd,
My old lady had 2 much booze last nite & ended up in the hospital. Come by 2nite, I need comradeship,

From,
The Reb
P.S. *What U.S. Prez with the first name of "Hiram" also loved booze?*

Jane Ann read the note for the fifth time in the dim light of Rebbie's front porch. "Ring the bell again, Lyddy," she said. "She's got to be here."

"I can't figure why she hasn't answered the phone all this time," Lydia said. She pressed her thumb on the doorbell. "Didn't she come home for dinner? It's been over two hours since we started calling." She shivered. "It's cold out! And Rebbie's house is creepy. I've always thought Rebbie's house was creepy."

Jane Ann folded the note and leaned against a wooden column. Rebbie's house was set far back from the street like a plantation in the old South. It was partly hidden by flanks of tall trees. The wooden porch that wound around the house carried sounds, amplified creaks and footfalls and scurrying noises from underneath.

"You're right. She's got to be here," Lydia said, tapping with her fingers on the door. "The bell's working—I heard it ring. And even if she went out, shouldn't the maid be here?" Lydia walked around the porch far enough to look in the living-

room windows. "Light's on," she said, "but nobody's there."

"If she's making fools out of us, I'll—" Jane
Ann broke off. "If my mother knew I was here,
she'd—"

"Look," said Lydia, "keep calm. You haven't
lied to your parents. They said you could sleep at
my house, right? And that's what you're going to
do. I'm not crazy about hanging around this place
either. When we find Rebbie we'll make her come
with us." Lydia motioned. "Let's walk around
back and see if there's a sign of anyone."

Jane Ann followed Lydia. A stiff breeze suddenly sent leaves skittering across the porch.
Dark branches waved as the two of them stood in
front of the living-room window, straining to see
through the gauzy curtains inside.

"They shouldn't have left her alone," Lydia
said.

"I know. Couldn't her father fly back tonight?"

"He likes to be away—that's what I think," Lydia said. "Maybe he thinks leaving Rebbie with
the maid is O.K., but Rebbie says Hildy takes extra time off. And Rebbie's brother—well, even
when he's here, he's no help. They had to bribe
him with a car to get him to go away to school. He
practically got kicked out of Windsor High." Lydia, keeping close to the siding, felt her way along
the front of the house. "Come on," she said.

Jane Ann walked behind her. "I wish we had a
flashlight."

"What I worry about," Lydia said in a low
voice, "is Rebbie doing something stupid. You
know what I mean—something *really* stupid."

Jane Ann looked at Lydia, but a heavy shadow
hid her face. "You mean hurting herself?"

Lydia nodded. "Rebbie puts on a big act that
she doesn't care about her parents, but when her
mother's sick, she gets really upset. I'm not saying
she'd go jump off a bridge or anything, but she
might do something stupid just to show her par-

ents, 'Look, I can shake you up, too!' Mummy had
a patient who tried to starve herself to get back at
her parents."

"At least we don't have to worry about *that*
with Rebbie," Jane Ann said. "Maybe we ought to
call the police if we can't find her, or get your
mother. Maybe we should get your mother right
now."

"Let's take a quick look ourselves since we're
right here," Lydia said.

A gust of wind through the evergreens whipped
the needles against the sides of the house like
giant paintbrushes.

"Do you hear something, Lyddy—whining or
humming? Music maybe?" Jane Ann put her ear
against the siding.

Lydia stood still and concentrated. "No," she
said. "Come around back." Lydia led the way
along a path of broken flagstones.

"Wait, Lyddy!" Jane Ann reached out to clear
aside shaggy, untrimmed branches. "Don't go
alone. It's so dark!" Over the sound of the trees
blowing, Jane Ann heard a tinkling noise.
"What's that?" Jane Ann came close to Lydia.
They cupped their hands around their ears.

"Glass?" Lydia said.

"Bottles, I bet!" Jane Ann remembered something she had noticed other times—a shopping
bag full of empty bottles by the garbage can.

"There's a light upstairs in Rebbie's room." Lydia pointed.

Jane Ann walked closer to the house. Under
Rebbie's window she heard a rhythmic clinking.
Something grazed her head. "Lydia! What is this
thing?" Jane Ann felt cold metal, a chain.

Lydia joined her, and the two of them clutched
awkwardly at whatever it was that swayed in the
wind.

"I know what it is!" Lydia said. "It's a safety
ladder. A metal ladder that you hook on a win-

dowsill and drop down as a fire escape. We have them for our third-floor room."

"Why does Rebbie have one?"

"For safety, I guess."

"You mean her father buys her a ladder for safety and then goes off and leaves her to maybe kill herself?" Jane Ann couldn't imagine it. She would expect the Haverds to have chain ladders— to write away for the best kind in some catalogue—but Mr. Hellerman with his fat cigars was the last person she'd imagine worrying about home safety.

"It does seem strange," Lydia said. "Go up, Jane Ann. Climb up and look in the window."

"To the top?" Jane Ann hesitated. She was secretly afraid of height. "*You* go," she said.

"Go on, you weigh less," Lydia nudged her. "I'll hold it steady."

Grasping the ladder with both hands, Jane Ann felt it become taut beneath her feet.

"Go on," Lydia said.

She went up one rung. The ladder quivered under her grip. Do it fast, she told herself, and the next steps came more easily.

"Keep going! Look in the window. Maybe she's asleep in her room." Lydia's face faded away in darkness.

Jane Ann felt a branch brush against her. The wind rose, cutting through her jacket and blowing up her sleeves. She was flying again, this time without a bicycle. She closed her eyes so she wouldn't have to look down. They were full of tears from the wind.

Suddenly the ladder, still attached at the windowsill, swung free at the bottom. Jane Ann clung fiercely as it dipped toward the house.

"It got away from me!" Lydia called. "Hang on, I'll grab it again."

"No, don't!" Jane Ann closed her eyes as the ladder bobbed back and forth. "It's better hanging free." *How is this thing fastened,* she wondered,

expecting to hear the crunch of splintering wood.
Which would be worse, falling from the top or
getting there and seeing that Rebbie had done
something really stupid? She couldn't believe Rebbie would hurt herself, but then, didn't Rebbie
often do dangerous things just for laughs? She
remembered Rebbie's horoscope for evening: *Be
daring.*

Now with every step the ladder buckled in toward the house. Jane Ann remembered her own
forecast and laughed under her breath. "Lyddy,"
she called, "My horoscope—*Keep aspirations high
in evening!*" She wanted to laugh and cry at the
same time, just as she had wanted to do outside
Mr. Turner's house. One more rung would put her
in a position to see Rebbie's room. She pulled herself up until she could grab the windowsill.

"What do you see?" Lydia called.

Jane Ann looked through the partly open window. On the wall the finger of Uncle Sam
pointed accusingly at her from an old poster. A
network of Japanese lanterns suspended from the
ceiling cast oblong shadows on the bare floor, and
a record revolved on the turntable. Maybe that
was the whining sound she had heard earlier.

"Do you see anything?" Lydia was impatient.

"No . . . no sign of Rebbie. . . . Unless . . ."
She studied the outline of the bed, the bunched-
up blankets.

"Nothing?" Lydia's voice rose insistently.
"Then come down."

"Just a minute." Flexing her stiff fingers and
gripping the ladder again, she held her breath and
watched for a shifting of blankets, but everything
was still. Two beer cans stood on the bedside table. "There's a big pile of blankets on the bed, I
think."

"Could it be Rebbie?"

The more Jane Ann looked, the more the blankets
seemed to take on Rebbie's lumpy form.

"I don't know," she answered. "I'm not sure."

"I'm coming up," Lydia shouted.

"Are you crazy? It'll break loose!" Jane Ann felt a tug and extra weight at the bottom. "Don't, Lyddy! Let me come down." She couldn't bear to look any more, couldn't stand the uncertainty of the lump under the covers. Turning away from the window, Jane Ann backed down as Lydia came up.

"Lyddy, you're being crazy," she yelled again. "It won't hold us both—you sent me up because I weigh less, remember?"

Lydia grabbed Jane Ann's ankle. "I have to see," she said. The chain ladder wobbled freakily. The two of them met in the middle.

"Hold it, Lyddy. Don't jiggle. What's that?"

They both held still. A strange sound rose over the wind.

"Good God." Lydia froze.

"What'll we do?"

"It's on the ground," Lydia said.

"It's a person," Jane Ann whispered. "Lyddy!"

Footsteps crackled under the trees.

"Jane Ann," Lydia tightened her grip around Jane Ann's ankle, "it's a maniac. When I say, 'One, two, three,' back down as fast as you can! Then jump and run! One . . . two . . . three!" At the signal the two of them backed down and leaped away from the ladder so that it hurtled through the air.

But neither of them ran. A dark form enveloped Lydia as she hit the ground. Lydia shrieked and Jane Ann fell over her. The two of them lay in a heap, pinned down by a heavy weight.

"No trespassing under penalty of death," said a ghostly voice that they knew, even in their panic, belonged to Rebbie.

"You vile, vile thing!" Lydia shouted, wiggling out from under.

"Typical!" Jane Ann sat up slowly.

"You know you're not funny, Rebbie," Lydia said.

"Hey," said Rebbie, painfully rising to her feet and extending a hand to pull Lydia up. "What're you, an oddball? *Everybody* thinks I'm funny!"

Lydia refused Rebbie's hand. "If your idea of funny is not answering your phone and doorbell for hours and finding two kids with broken necks in your backyard, then I agree, you're very funny."

Rebbie laughed nervously. "I guess I have a weird sense of humor. Are you mad at me too, Jannie? What do you say?"

"I say Ulysses S. Grant. Hiram Ulysses Grant." Jane Ann got up. The three of them stood together under the porch roof.

"What? What did you say?" Lydia asked.

"The U.S. President who loved booze!" Jane Ann said. "The answer to Rebbie's question at the end of her note. President Grant was given at birth the name Hiram, but he changed it and used his middle name, Ulysses."

Lydia groaned. "You're both crazy!"

"The only way to get back at Rebbie," said Jane Ann, "is to beat her at her own game."

"Who needs two insane friends?" Lydia buried her face in her hands.

"Come on inside," Rebbie invited, punching each of them lightly on the arm. "Let's face it, we need each other."

6

Rebbie, bumping along in the dark, led the way up the steps. She groped for the light inside the door, and when she had flicked it on, the three of them surveyed the large modern kitchen. On the formica countertop lay a plate from the delicatessen covered with plastic wrap.

"I guess that was my supper," Rebbie said, lifting off the wrap, dangling a slice of roast beef and lowering it into her mouth. "I see Hildy slaved over a hot stove all day. That's why she had to take the evening off—she wore herself out! Anybody hungry?" She held out the plate. Jane Ann and Lydia shook their heads.

"Didn't you eat?" Lydia stood with her arms folded in front of her.

"Yes, Mummy, I ate," Rebbie mocked. "Of course I didn't zip down to my local back-to-nature store for shredded lettuce on whole wheat like the wholesome Haverds eat."

Lydia started to say something, but she held off.

"I ate a whole pizza by myself, if you want to know," Rebbie went on, "and two bottles of non-diet soda. That ought to make me big and strong, don't you think, Mummy Lydia?" Rebbie, chomping on a large slice of pickle, looked at them defiantly.

"Rebbie," Lydia said in a shaky voice.

Jane Ann leaned on the counter. "Reb, where have you been all this time?"

"And how's your mother?" Lydia asked.

"Question number one," said Rebbie. She sat down on a stool by the counter and sampled cole slaw with her fingers. "I've been all over this town today—the hospital, the astrology shop, the pizza joint. Just now I was lying in my room waiting for you, listening to music."

"Didn't you hear the doorbell?"

"I thought I heard something, but when I came to the door nobody was there."

"We must have just gone around the back," Jane Ann said.

"So I walked out on the porch," Rebbie continued. "I heard strange voices around the back, and I found these two perverts climbing up to spy on me—"

"Rebbie! Hey, how's your mother?" Lydia insisted.

"By now she's probably ready to come home and start all over again."

"Is she going to be O.K.?" Jane Ann asked.

"The doctors think so—when her clothes dry out. Hey, you don't know what she did last night. She threw all her clothes in the bathtub! Man, you should've seen her fur coat."

"All her clothes?" Lydia asked.

"Yeah." Rebbie laughed. "And my father's clothes—outasight! She must have thought she was running a laundromat. The booze hit her in a certain way. She started thinking everything was dirty. Man, I wish she'd at least have used cold-water soap so the stuff wouldn't shrink. Shrink . . ." Rebbie repeated. "Ha! That's where she is now. At the shrink. The analyst. The *county hospital.*"

"How did you get her there?" Jane Ann asked.

"When she was doing all these weird things, I called Dr. Karl. You've met Dr. Karl. You know, he's this friend of my parents, our doctor. He came over, took one look at her, and called the ambulance. She didn't want to go, but they took her. I said, 'Keep her here,' but Dr. Karl called my old man in Chicago, and my old man said, 'What, again? Keep her in the hospital till tomorrow when I come home.' 'Let me at least go with her,' I said, so Dr. Karl drove me to the hospital real late. When I got there she was asleep, so I went to sleep too, in the visitors' lounge. Dr. Karl said I had to go to school this morning, but when he dropped me there, I didn't feel like staying. I called guidance from the booth outside school. I disguised my voice and told the secretary, 'Rebecca Hellerman has an emergency.' Isn't that a crock?"

Lydia studied Rebbie's face. "Why did you cut school?"

"I was beat from sleeping on a couch, plus I wanted to check horoscopes. God, horoscopes!" Rebbie leaped up. "Jannie, did you get the part?"

"Yeah, I got it."

"See? What did I tell you! I knew it! Terrific!" Rebbie finished off the contents of the paper plate and tossed it in the garbage. "Jannie, now— admit it—did I know what I was talking about?"

Jane Ann nodded. "It looks like it. Things keep happening. *Keep aspirations high*—that's what mine says for this evening. That's why I was up on your safety ladder."

"Yeah!" Rebbie laughed. "You made it all the way to the top of that spastic ladder? I wouldn't trust a rag doll on that thing."

"Isn't it for safety?" Lydia asked.

"It's for letting my brother out at night when he's home for the weekend. So my parents won't know."

"At *your* window?"

"Isn't he shrewd?" Rebbie said. "Isn't he artfully devious, as Hugh Turner would say?"

"Does your brother really use the ladder?" Jane Ann remembered the clammy touch of cold metal.

"Last time it came unhooked and he landed in the bushes."

"Then you mean we could have . . ." Jane Ann

glanced at the kitchen clock. "Hey, Lydia, we'd better be going."

"Going where?" Rebbie blocked their way. "You just got here."

"Going to my house," Lydia said. "Are you all alone, Reb?"

"Yeah. Hildy's not supposed to leave, but she took off for the evening. She'll be back."

"And your brother—didn't he come home?" Jane Ann stared absently at a remnant of roast beef that had missed the garbage and clung to the side of the bag.

"No, what's the use? The old lady'll be home tomorrow. Poor kid—he always misses the best scenes." The three of them looked at one another in silence. "Hey, come on," Rebbie said, "don't get gloomy. Let's be congenial companions. That's my word for the day. Come up to my room and listen to music."

"We can't," Jane Ann said, nudging Lydia for support. "My parents think I'm at Lyddy's, and—"

"And they wouldn't approve of your hanging around here?"

"No, that's not it. . . ." Jane Ann twisted a button on her jacket.

Lydia sat down on a stool next to Rebbie's. "Rebbie, come to my house tonight. Please. Call Dr. Karl. Leave Hildy a note."

"I wanted you two to stay here." Rebbie said quietly.

"We *can't*. Come with us," Lydia said again. "My mother insists. She wants you to come."

"No, thanks. I'm staying here." Rebbie turned away from them. "Fine friends you two are."

There was a misery in Rebbie's eyes, Jane Ann thought, a sign of something a hundred times worse than the Scary Feeling. Jane Ann hesitated. "If we come up to your room for a while, will you sleep over at Lydia's? All our stuff is over there, and—"

Rebbie sighed. "All right, all right—but come

up and listen to this." She slid off the stool. "I just feel like being in my house."

They climbed the thickly-carpeted stairs, and Jane Ann looked at the framed photographs of Mr. Hellerman that hung on the wall, shots of him posing with various businessmen and politicians, always with a cigar in his mouth. Rebbie led them to her room at the top of the curving staircase. The turntable was still spinning, the blankets heaped on the bed.

"I thought that was *you* before," Jane Ann said. She sat on the bed and punched the blankets down until they lay flat.

"Even *I'm* not that deformed!" Rebbie stopped the turntable and lifted the record. "Get comfortable, kids. This is what I want you to hear. My brother gave me this record. I play it over and over. He says everybody used to freak out over this. I mean when she was a big star—when she was alive." Rebbie held up the album cover. "I really dig Janis Joplin," she said. Rebbie rejected the record and moved the needle to the second band.

The words of the first band died out, and the guitar introduction to *Me and Bobby McGee* began. Rebbie slouched against the wall. Lydia stretched out on the window seat. Jane Ann stared first at the picture of Janis on the album cover and then at Rebbie. For once she could get a good look at Rebbie. Reb, eyes closed, was loose, relaxed. Janis Joplin's voice made you feel like letting loose, Jane Ann thought. Naturally Rebbie would admire a person like Janis. That's what Rebbie herself wanted to be—free, loose. Freedom, Janis was singing, is having nothing left to lose. Jane Ann, tapping her foot soundlessly, wished she could let loose, wished she could take more leaps, more risks, like Rebbie. What made her feel roped in, Jane Ann wondered, like a plant tied to a stake? Was it her parents and their rules, or some leash she put on herself that kept her from doing whatever she felt like doing? *When I'm in a play, I'm different,* she reminded herself. Why couldn't she feel free in real life? "Bobby McGee—aaahhh . . ." Rebbie howled at the exuberant end of the song.

Rebbie lifted the needle. "Want to hear it again? She's the greatest."

"Wouldn't you rather listen to somebody who's popular *now*?" Lydia asked. "Somebody who's alive?"

"No," Rebbie said. She laid the arm of the phonograph to rest. "The best people are dead."

"Rebbie!" Jane Ann sat up straight on the bed. "That's a stupid thing to say!"

"It's true," Rebbie's voice was flat.

Lydia looked out the window and said nothing.

"What do you mean? Who are the *best* people?" Jane Ann challenged.

"Janis Joplin," Rebbie said tonelessly. "She's dead. Humphrey Bogart's dead. President John F. Kennedy's dead. So are thirty-five other American Presidents—a few crummy ones, but most of them good. W. C. Fields is dead, and Shakespeare . . ." Rebbie went on cataloging losses.

"Well, naturally," Jane Ann said impatiently, "but nobody you knew personally. What about us—Lyddy and me? We're alive. Don't we count?"

Rebbie nodded. "Yeah," she said wearily. "The best people are dead, all except you two."

Lydia came over to her and rested a hand on her arm. "Rebbie, you've had a bad time. Maybe it was bad enough to make you think nobody cares about you. But that's not true. We've been trying like anything to reach you. I care. Jane Ann cares. So do other people."

Jane Ann could see that Rebbie was struggling to believe what Lydia was saying. No wonder Rebbie was depressed. She had watched her own mother falling apart, being carried off to a hospital.

"Come to my house, Rebbie," Lydia was saying.

"Bring your album. We'll listen to the rest of it, and then you'll get a good night's sleep."

Lydia was good with people, Jane Ann thought. Lydia would be able to handle Rebbie. Even now Reb was looking more like her old self.

"Will you both do something for me?" Rebbie asked. Her voice came out thin and breathless.

"Yes," Jane Ann said. She slipped down onto the floor. The three of them, cross-legged, formed a triangle. "What?"

"Make a pact," said Rebbie.

"A pact?" Lydia exchanged a look with Jane Ann.

"A friendship pact."

"Sure," Jane Ann shrugged. "How do we do it?"

Rebbie's eyes glistened. "We cross arms and make a friendship circle, and we swear that whenever any one of us is in trouble, the other two have to stand by. No quitting."

Lydia nodded.

"And to seal the pact," Rebbie went on, "we do truth-and-consequences."

"How does that go?" Jane Ann asked.

"To prove we trust each other," Rebbie said, "we each tell a truth—something personal we've never said before—and then we each make up a consequence—a dare that we all do together."

"What's the point?" Lydia asked. "We can trust each other without that."

"That's the pact." Rebbie's voice was edgy, final.

"Well, O.K.," Lydia said slowly. "Let's do it."

"Hold on like this." Rebbie linked their hands. "Repeat after me," she said.

Jane Ann felt Lydia's cool, slim fingers in her left hand and Rebbie's damp grip on her right.

"I solemnly swear," Rebbie waited for them to repeat, ". . . to help my two best friends . . . in time of trouble . . . and to follow the trail of friendship . . . wherever it leads."

Lydia and Jane Ann echoed the last phrase.

"Good," Rebbie said. "Very good." She let go. "Now, the truth."

"You go first," Lydia said.

"All right, I will." Rebbie's face was flushed. Damp curls strayed out of the elastic band that gathered her hair together in the back. It struck Jane Ann that Rebbie looked a little bit like Janis Joplin on the album cover.

"The truth." Rebbie shifted her weight and cleared her throat. "The truth," she repeated in a shrill, unnatural voice, "is that the mood I'm in, I don't give a damn about anybody in this world— except you two. My parents would be glad if I were dead, like those people I mentioned." She took a breath and went on quickly. "I drank two and a half cans of beer before you came, and I decided if you didn't show up at all, I'd swallow that bottle of pills over there by my bed." She laughed nervously.

Jane Ann saw the brown bottle. Her eyes filled up and she felt her heart pounding in her ear. Lydia was right. Rebbie *could* do something really stupid. It was lucky that they had come when they had.

"Rebbie," Lydia said, "we *came*. You should have known we'd come." She put an arm around Rebbie's shoulder.

Jane Ann rocked back and forth in her cross-legged position. She felt tied up, as usual. Why couldn't she reach out and comfort people the way Lydia could? Lydia was smoothing back the stray wisps of Rebbie's hair and rewinding the elastic. Jane Ann, hugging her knees, felt useless.

"Thanks," Rebbie said to Lydia. Then she pulled away from her. "It's great to have true friends," she said formally. "Now the test—the consequence—the ordeal, as they called it in medieval times. Stay where you are."

Rebbie hoisted herself up and left the room.

Jane Ann and Lydia looked at each other as Rebbie thumped down the carpeted stairs.

"What did I tell you?" Lydia whispered.

"What do you think she's doing?"

Lydia strained to listen. "I don't know, but we'd better go along with it." Lydia looked at her watch. "Let's give her another fifteen minutes and then get her out of here."

Footsteps came closer, and Rebbie was back in the room. She carried a liquor bottle and three little glasses.

"No, Rebbie." Jane Ann made a face as soon as she saw her. "No, I hate the taste."

"Wait!" Rebbie set down the bottle and joined them to form the triangle again. "It's not what you think. I'm not trying to get you smashed, to mess you up. This is something special—a ceremony, and I only want you to wet your lips."

Jane Ann looked at the bottle with the picture of a southern plantation on the label. *Southern Comfort,* it said.

"First, to Janis Joplin," Rebbie said as she handed each of them a heavy-bottomed little glass.

"Did she drink this?" Jane Ann asked. She pressed the dense, cool glass against her forehead, then set it on the floor.

"Yes." Rebbie kneeled and poured three glasses. Then she put the phonograph needle back on the record. It was eerie, Jane Ann thought, toasting to someone who was dead, someone whose voice, so full of life, was all around you.

> *Trust in me, baby . . .*
> *Give me time, give me time—*
> *I heard somebody say . . .*
> *The older the grape, the sweeter*
> *the wine . . .* *

* Lyrics from *Trust Me* by Bobby Womack. Copyright © 1967 Metric Music Company/Tracebob Music Co. Used by permission.

Rebbie lifted her glass. "To Janis," she said. Lydia raised hers slowly to her lips.

Jane Ann clasped both hands around her glass and stared at it. "I think in memory of her we should throw it down the sink," she said. "It killed her, didn't it?"

Rebbie shook her head. "Janis Joplin died from drugs, not this. Anyway," she said patiently, "when you hold a memorial, you should do what the person would have wanted." Rebbie tapped her glass. "This is how she would have wanted to be remembered. Plus this is also to our friendship. You're doing this for *me*."

Lydia tilted the glass and sipped steadily.

"Jannie?" Rebbie said, waiting. "To Janis Joplin, to Jannie getting the part in the play, to our friendship, and to *Hugh*."

Jane Ann lifted the glass and touched it to her mouth. She let first one drop, then another trickle down her throat. It burned and left her lips and throat tingling and numb.

Rebbie smiled. "Good enough! You passed the ordeal." She took the glass from Jane Ann and added the leftover contents to her own. With a quick glance at each of them, she finished it in one swallow.

"Rebbie!" Lydia shouted.

"Ugh." Jane Ann felt like gagging.

"There!" said Rebbie. "To Janis Joplin and to friendship. Tell us a truth now, Jannie."

Jane Ann squirmed. Her first impulse was to say, "The truth is, Rebbie, half the time I love you better than a sister and the other half you disgust me, and right now I feel both things at once," but she didn't say it.

"Well, come on."

"What about?" Jane Ann hesitated. "What kind of truth?"

"Oh, who you like . . . what's the worst thing you can think of . . . stuff like that."

"I like . . ." Jane Ann saw images of faces in

her mind. "I like . . . you two . . . and Neil Delancy . . ." Rebbie nodded encouragement. "And
Mr. Turner . . ." Jane Ann stopped. "I *love*
Hugh Turner." She said it fast and too loud. Rebbie smiled. "And the worst thing I can think of
is—is losing all that. Losing you two and never
seeing Neil or Mr. Turner again. And losing my
part in the play. That's all." She sat back and
breathed quickly.

"Good," Rebbie said, "a good truth." She
swayed forward dizzily as if to pat Jane Ann on
the back, but suddenly she lost her balance and
toppled over on her side.

"Rebbie, are you all right?" Lydia grabbed her
shoulders, tried to sit her up. Jane Ann knelt
down close to Rebbie's face. The flush had disappeared from her cheeks. Rebbie was white. Beads
of perspiration stood out on her forehead and her
upper lip.

"Oohhhh, goddam!" Rebbie roared. "I'm going
to be sick. Let me up!" She uncurled her body and
got to her feet. "Help!" She stumbled over Jane
Ann and dashed for the bathroom.

Lydia ran behind her. Jane Ann followed.

"Oohhhh . . ." Rebbie, kneeling on the floor
over the toilet bowl, leaned on Lydia.

"Take it easy, Reb," said Jane Ann, offering
support on the other side.

"It came over me all of a sudden," she moaned.
"I want to die!" She heaved, lurching forward.
Jane Ann grabbed her firmly by the elbow as Lydia steered her head. The retching and the long
gush left Rebbie gasping, panting for breath.

"It's all right, Rebbie," Lydia said. "Get rid of
it. Do it again." The gargling sound was followed
by a second gush, and Rebbie pulled away. Lydia
reached for a washcloth. "It's all right, Rebbie,"
she said. "That's what friends are for."

"Don't worry, Reb," Jane Ann said, turning her
face as she flushed the toilet.

"I'm such a jerk." Rebbie, hiding her wet face,

curled up in a heap on the bathroom floor. "I'm so revolting," she repeated between sobs. "I'm such a slob!"

"It's O.K., Rebbie," Jane Ann said.

The two of them sat by her, and Lydia, turning Rebbie's head around, laid a wet washcloth on her forehead.

Rebbie slapped the washcloth down so that it hid her face. "I should never have eaten that cole slaw," she said.

Jane Ann and Lydia looked at each other.

"Come on, Rebbie," Lydia patted her gently, "I'm going to call my mother to come for us."

"I'm too sick."

"You'll feel better after my mother gives you an Alka-Seltzer and tucks you in."

"I can't even raise my head," she shuddered.

Lydia looked at Jane Ann.

"Come on, Rebbie," Lydia urged. "A cup of tea?"

"Yecch! Leave me for dead." She rolled over.

Jane Ann thought for a second. Lydia's calm touch wasn't working. Jane Ann tapped Rebbie on the ankle. "Hey," she said, "which three-time loser for the Presidency of the U.S. supposedly died as a result of *overeating*?"

Rebbie twitched and turned over slowly. She raised her head and looked at Jane Ann. Her hair hung limp and matted, her shirt was wrinkled and stained.

"Too easy," she whispered. "You'll have to do better than that to stump the Reb." She smiled weakly. "William Jennings Bryan. Died in 1925."

"Now let's get out of here," said Lydia, standing up and pulling Rebbie to her feet before she could protest. "The trail of friendship leads to my house."

7

A chilly breeze blew in the partly open casement window, and Jane Ann crept down farther under the covers. The Haverds' attic—the third-floor room they called their dormitory—sprawled across the entire house and sloped at the ends. Trunks and stored furniture loomed like sleeping ghosts in the corners. But with Lydia in the other single, and with Rebbie under a pile of blankets in the double bed, Jane Ann in her own four-poster felt protected. Classical music floated up from below.

What a day. She should have been dead tired, but fragments tumbling in her head like bits of glass in a kaleidoscope kept her tossing uncomfortably: Brightburn's rhinestone-studded glasses; the yellow playbook; the golden sleekness of Lyddy's live model; the silver ladder; the numbing amber of Southern Comfort. They had never finished Rebbie's friendship pact, she remembered.

"Rebbie. *All the best people are dead, except you two.* Jane Ann pulled the pillow over her head, let her arms and legs go limp, and tried to imagine what it would be like to be dead. She held her breath as long as she could, until her ribs felt as if they would pop up one by one. It was no use though—death was beyond her imagining. What attracted Rebbie to it? And was Rebbie's talk about pills serious, or just another one of her sick jokes to get attention?

In the big bed a few feet away from her, Jane Ann heard Rebbie roll over and sigh in her sleep.

She pictured again Rebbie's room as she had seen it through the window, with the heap on the bed that might have been a person.

What if it had been? Jane Ann imagined herself crawling through the window, shaking Rebbie and slapping her face to wake her, telephoning for an ambulance. She pictured Rebbie afterward, pale and white-robed in a hospital, ashamed and grateful. "I'll never forget it was you who saved my life," the imaginary Rebbie whispered. Then Jane Ann tried out a tragic ending: Rebbie's body heavy and motionless under the blanket . . . mouth agape . . . her own face buried in the covers and her own voice sobbing too late, "Why did you do it, Rebbie? We loved you!"

Make the night go fast, she told herself. Think of pleasant things. Think of *Our Town*. Think of Neil in the part of George Gibbs and how he had looked when he congratulated her on playing Emily. Shy Neil who would be marrying her in the play. Marrying her and after that becoming a widower when the character Emily died in childbirth. Death—even in the play! *Especially* in the play, since the whole third act took place in a graveyard. She couldn't escape it. Maybe if she said the word a hundred times she'd get it out of her head. Death, death, death, death . . . Ridiculous. That didn't help. What would?

Imagine—imagine the most impossibly wonderful thing. Something about Mr. Turner. Mr. Turner directing her in a Broadway play. No, something more personal. Mr. Turner marrying her in real life. But Mr. Turner was already married. In fact, his wife was expecting a baby. Well, in daydreams anything could happen. Jane Ann plumped up the pillow and stuck it under her head. She stretched out in bed and pictured the future—maybe ten years from now: Mr. Turner's wife would have an incurable illness. The doctors would have tried everything. Then one day Mr. Turner would run into Jane Ann on the street.

"Jannie! You're so grown up!" She would smile confidently because of all the experience she had gotten in the meantime. Mrs. Turner would die—quickly and painlessly—and Mr. Turner would discover he was in love with Jane Ann. People would say, "He's so old for you!" But "The older the grape, the sweeter the wine," she would tell them. Soon the same people would be pointing to her and saying, "Isn't it beautiful how she's raised his child as her own?"

Jane Ann yawned and smiled in the dark. The fantasy was stupid, she knew, and selfish, since it meant killing off Mrs. Turner. Still, it had made her sleepy. The music from below faded away, and a door closed in the room beneath her. She floated in a fuzzy gray space between sleep and waking. Lydia, on the other side of the dormitory, slept soundly. Suddenly the double bed began to creak.

"Hey, Jannie . . ." Rebbie rolled over on her side with a snort, like a hippo in the mud. "You awake?"

"Nnnn . . . barely."

"It's hot as hell in here!" Rebbie tossed again and threw the covers off.

"I'm cold," Jane Ann whispered faintly.

"Well, one of us must be crazy then. Probably me as usual." Rebbie sat upright. "Were you asleep?"

"I was about to be," Jane Ann said. Drowsiness ebbed away.

"Talk to me for a minute, Jannie. I woke up because I'm *so hot!*"

Jane Ann was stricken with a hopeless feeling that she wouldn't sleep all night, would go to her first rehearsal tomorrow stumbling and dimwitted, with dark circles under her eyes. "Go ahead," she said in a monotone, "talk."

"We never finished the friendship pact."

"I know."

"We can do it tomorrow."

"We don't need that stuff to be friends, Reb."

"You said you would." Rebbie's voice quavered.

"Well, we would've done it if you hadn't . . ." *made a pig of yourself,* Jane Ann was about to say. ". . . if you hadn't gotten sick," she finished. "Are you O.K. now?"

"I'm weak."

"You looked miserable." Jane Ann pictured again Rebbie's damp forehead, her neck thrust forward in agony. "Lyddy was good though. She always knows what to do."

"Is Lyddy asleep?"

"Yeah."

"Lyddy annoys me sometimes."

Jane Ann stiffened. "What do you mean?" Jane Ann asked cautiously. Some part of her, she had to admit, wanted to hear criticism of Lydia.

"She and her whole family are so damned perfect," Rebbie carped.

Jane Ann smiled. She was glad it was dark so Rebbie couldn't see her. It was true—the Haverds *were* so damned perfect. Still, was that bad? "So what's wrong with being perfect?" she asked.

"It's boring," Rebbie said.

"How do you mean?" Jane Ann stifled a laugh.

"Lydia's always prepared," Rebbie went on. "Her mother never gets upset. I always know exactly what they're going to do before they do it. It's so *boring!*"

"Shush, Rebbie! Lydia might hear you!"

"So what, it's the truth."

"It's not fair to knock the Haverds when you're in their house, when they're being nice to you." Jane Ann felt divided. Lyddy was a best friend, but cattiness was fun.

"I'm not knocking," Rebbie said. "It just bugs me when I can predict what a person's going to do. I'd tell Lyddy to her face."

"But it's good that the Haverds handle everything so well," Jane Ann argued. "I wish I could be that way." She remembered her face getting red at the art studio.

"You're better the way you are," Rebbie said. "Lyddy makes people feel inferior. Not on purpose," Rebbie continued, "but it's just the way her whole family is. They have this perfect setup. Father a dignified professor with hot-shot manners. Mother with an important job, not just some sloppy, boozing housewife. Kids all talented and clean-cut. Books and magazines up to your ass in every room—even the bathroom. Magazines that tell you what movies you're supposed to like, books that tell you how to quit smoking, guides that tell you to buy a Volvo that'll last a hundred years." Rebbie sniffed. "And *discussions!* Discussions from breakfast straight through to dinner— 'Is there life on Mars?' 'Which is healthier, soybeans or alfalfa?' I can't even remember when my old man and old lady sat down together at the dinner table last."

"You're just jealous," Jane Ann said quietly.

"No, I'm not!" Rebbie said. "I wouldn't *want* to be a Haverd. It would be *boring*. You just *know* that Lyddy and her brothers are going to go to good colleges like Greenmore, and marry professors and doctors, and have more smart kids just like them, and read about how to raise their kids in a pollution-free environment, and—oh, forget it!" Rebbie broke off. "All that's why Lyddy is my second best friend."

"Second best?"

"Yeah, you dope," Rebbie shouted, "*second best!*"

"Shhhh!" Jane Ann warned.

Rebbie lowered her voice. "Jannie, don't wish you were like Lydia," she said. "You're more fun. You're more unpredictable—a Pisces. That means your nature contains many possibilities and many facets. I read that somewhere. I like that."

"But the *three* of us—" Jane Ann protested.

"Look," Rebbie went on, "I like Lydia a lot.

She'll always help me out like she did tonight. I know that. I can *predict* that. But you're better. I count more on you."

"You do?"

"Yeah, because . . . Look, let's face it. Lyddy's *set*. She won't ever really need either one of us, right? Let's you and me make a pact."

Jane Ann drew back. "Leave Lyddy out?" She looked across at the single bed, half expecting Lydia to sit up and catch them.

"Well, our own two-party agreement," Rebbie said. "No more truth and consequences. Just promise that you and me'll never quit on each other."

"I won't quit." Jane Ann remembered her fantasy of saving Rebbie's life. "And you wouldn't do anything stupid, would you, Reb? I mean . . ." she hesitated. "You wouldn't really swallow those pills?"

The room was quiet except for the creaking of the double bed.

"Not if you swear," Rebbie said finally. "Friendship forever, O.K?" She reached across the gap between their beds, grabbed Jane Ann's hand, and gripped it tightly. "Leo and Pisces forever," she said.

Jane Ann hesitated. "O.K." She returned the grip. That was the least she could do. She wasn't sure exactly what she was promising, but the last thing Rebbie needed right now was friends running out on her, people saying no. "It's still you, me, and Lyddy, though, isn't it?" Jane Ann said, half a statement, half a question.

"Yeah," Rebbie yawned. "You, Lyddy, me, and my Bobby McGee! Wooo! Man, I'm fatigued! I'm really wiped out. Thank God it's not so hot anymore." She rolled over and yanked up the blankets. "Good night."

"Good night." Jane Ann closed her eyes. Tomorrow she'd talk to Rebbie, straighten out a few things. Tell her she didn't want to gossip about

Lyddy anymore. Tomorrow she'd get Rebbie to throw away the pills. But now she was disappearing into the fuzzy, gray, half-asleep place.

"Jannie?"

At first Jane Ann thought the voice was in her dreams.

"Psssst, Jannie . . ." she heard again, low but persistent. She pretended to be asleep.

"Hey, answer in the name of Hugh Turner!"

"What!" Jane Ann sat up.

"Who assassinated President William McKinley, and how do you spell the assassin's name?"

"Rebbie!" Jane Ann churned. "Wake me up again, and I'll call Brightburn and tell her about the sex book! Now shut up and good night!"

8

"Jane Ann, wake up! We overslept." Lydia was leaning over her, tapping her shoulder. "It's quarter to eight," Lydia whispered. "Hurry up or we'll be late for school. My mother says to let Rebbie sleep. She'll see that Rebbie gets home later when her mother comes home."

"Lydia?" Jane Ann blinked.

"Yes?"

"Lydia?" Jane Ann sat up. Had she really stayed up talking to Rebbie, or had that been another fantasy? "Lyddy—did you—sleep O.K.?"

Lydia shrugged. "Sure, did you?"

"You didn't hear anything?"

"What," she smiled, "maniacs in the attic?"

Jane Ann felt guilty. Could Lydia guess from her expression that they had been talking about her behind her back? "No, forget it," she said. "I'll get up now."

"Meet me in the kitchen, Jane Ann. Mummy started breakfast, but we'll be lucky if we have time for orange juice. Don't make the bed, we're late—and don't wake Rebbie!" Lydia ran downstairs.

Jane Ann stepped onto the bare floor, took her jeans from the bedpost and slipped out of the nightgown she had borrowed from Lydia. Staying over at the Haverds' on a school night made everything confused. What day was it, anyway? Friday—the day of her first rehearsal. Where was everybody? Rebbie was in the double bed, probably dreaming of Franklin Delano Roosevelt. Mrs. Haverd was making breakfast. Dr. Haverd must still be sleeping, and the boys had probably gone out jogging.

In her own house, she thought, her mother would be giving Beth a bath in the little plastic tub right now. Her father would be about to leave for the office. Even though she'd only been gone twenty-four hours, she missed them. It was weird the way you could be so annoyed at parents and then feel sad just because you weren't going to see them at breakfast. The argument with them seemed as if it had happened a long time ago. *Please,* she thought, as she pulled on her clothes, *a good horoscope for today. And let Rebbie's mother be all right.* Throwing her belongings into a canvas bag, she tiptoed past Rebbie and headed down to the bathroom.

The Haverds' rambling house was like a fun house, with lots of passages and mysterious doors. The second-floor hallway was cool and silent as Jane Ann paused at the bottom of the attic steps and debated which bathroom to use. The modern one next to Mr. and Mrs. Haverd's room was the closest. She fumbled for her comb.

Jane Ann paused outside the bathroom. The

door was closed. She had already lifted her hand to knock when she stopped short. There was a strange sound inside, as if someone were crying. She put her ear to the door. A loud sob made her back away. She looked for a place to hide, stepped into the guest room. Had she imagined it? Tiptoeing into the hall again, Jane Ann strained to listen. Uncontrolled sobs rose and fell. But who was it— a guest in the house?

Jane Ann stood still. Stupid! she told herself, go to the other bathroom! But curiosity held her, an urge something like the one that had kept her tuned in to Rebbie's gossip about Lydia. Finding out who was crying seemed worth the risk of being caught listening at the door. Then the bathroom faucet gushed and something dropped onto the tile floor. Jane Ann jumped and made her way to the boys' bathroom at the other end of the hall.

Turning on the water in the sink full force, she splashed it in her face. Who was crying? Maybe Lydia *had* overheard Rebbie and her gossiping, and it had really hurt her feelings. *I'll make it up to her somehow*, Jane Ann told herself. She finished her preparations and walked into the hall again.

Almost at once she saw someone coming out of the modern bathroom. In the shadows of the hallway Jane Ann could see that it was a woman and her face was red and swollen. Her hair hung loose and wild. Jane Ann stood absolutely still. It was Mrs. Haverd. Calm, controlled, perfect *Mrs. Haverd.* Jane Ann walked fast toward the stairs.

"Oh!" Mrs. Haverd said, pretending to brush away something in her eye. "Oh, Jane Ann, you startled me!"

"Good morning," Jane Ann mumbled, but Mrs. Haverd didn't answer. Instead she went into her bedroom and closed the door. Jane Ann continued down the steps to the first floor.

Mrs. Haverd. Jane Ann felt dazed as she

walked through the dining room to the kitchen.
Mrs. Haverd! What could there be for someone
like Mrs. Haverd to cry about? Well, Rebbie must
be wrong. There wasn't any such thing as a perfect setup. Nobody could always be predicted. And
if *Mrs. Haverd* lost control, then *nothing* was absolutely for certain in this weirdo world.

"Do you tell your mother how you really feel,
Jane Ann—I mean about personal things?" Lydia
broke the silence as the two of them turned onto
Windsor Boulevard a block from the school.

It was a relief that Lydia was finally saying
something. An unseen third person had seemed to
be walking between them from the Haverds'
house. An invisible Rebbie or an invisible Mrs.
Haverd.

"I guess I don't tell my mother much," Jane
Ann said. "I'd like to, but—"

"Well, *I do*!" Lydia's voice rose sharply. "I tell
Mummy how I feel about everything. And except
for things she can't tell me because of being unprofessional, I always thought she'd tell *me* anything, too. But she won't."

"What do you mean?" Jane Ann looked straight
ahead.

"Something's wrong and she won't tell me."

"How do you know?"

"She was very upset this morning. She left the
breakfast table before you came down."

"Do you know why?"

Lydia shook her head. "I asked her what was
wrong and she wouldn't tell me. Don't you think
that's unfair? 'Talk about your problems—it
helps,' that's what Mummy always tells *me*.
That's what her job is—helping families talk
about their problems. Talking's supposed to help
everybody but her!" Lydia said angrily.

Jane Ann stopped walking. "I've never heard
you get mad at your mother before."

"Well, you're hearing me now! She's being hypocrite. My parents always say, 'Practice what you preach!' "

"She probably just wanted privacy. Your mother's got as much right as anybody else to cry in the bathroom," Jane Ann said before she could catch herself.

"You heard her?"

Jane Ann nodded. "I know what you mean. It's awful to see an adult cry. Especially_ *your* mother!" Jane Ann said. "You may think this sounds awful, but I'm almost glad your mother cried, because I always thought your family was—well, I thought nothing ever went wrong. I'm glad I'm finding out you're normal."

"We're normal all right. We're *always* arguing," Lydia bragged.

"That's an exaggeration. You know, you're really lucky, Lyddy. Rebbie'd probably say your life is balanced because you're a Libra. I don't know if that has anything to do with it, but you *are* lucky," Jane Ann said. "I mean, parents you can usually talk to, neat older brothers, your art lessons. . . ."

"I guess so," Lydia admitted.

"Sometimes I feel like things are tough for me," Jane Ann said. "You know—hassles with parents, wanting Neil to call, feeling shy. . . . But when I really think about it, I'm lucky, too. I've got the part in the play, and even if I don't tell 'truths' to my parents like I tell you and Reb, well, I love them and they love me. Look at Rebbie, what's *she* got at home?"

"I know. What do you think is going to happen to Mrs. Hellerman? Rebbie's trying to act cool about her troubles, but I don't know . . . those pills by her bed. . . . Do you think she'd feel better if we finished the pact?"

Jane Ann hesitated. "Lets not bring it up unless she does." She was sure now that Lydia hadn't heard the talk about a two-party agreement. "I've got a rehearsal after school," Jane Ann said, "but let's go see Rebbie tonight. She might be feeling down."

"Will your parents let you out?"

Jane Ann kicked a stone along the path to the main entrance of the school. "Who cares?" she said. "I'll go anyway. *Nobody's* telling me to keep away from Rebbie."

"Good," Lydia said as she opened the door. "Because Rebbie's counting on both of us."

Jane Ann swallowed hard. "Right," she said.

"You know," Lydia linked arms as they hurried down the hall to homeroom, "all three of us are lucky. It's unusual for three people to be so close. It's great to know you've got two friends who'll stand by you forever, isn't it?"

9

"We'll be here forever," Mr. Turner called, "unless everybody's on cue."

Phyllis Cooper rushed onstage.

"*Unless everybody's on cue*," he repeated from the apron of the stage. "Move further downstage, Phyllis. That's it. Take your line again, Neil."

Jane Ann liked the way Neil said his lines. His voice was gentle.

"That's good, Jannie," Mr. Turner broke in, "that's a nice touch with your hand like that. Keep that. O.K.," Mr. Turner said, "maybe this is a good stopping place for today." He swiveled around to face the rest of the cast in the first two rows of the auditorium. "You're good," he said. He waved Jane Ann, Neil, and Phyllis down from the stage and waited for them to take seats.

"Now it may seem as if our opening in January

is far off," he said, "but it isn't." Mr. Turner sat
down on the edge of the stage with his feet hanging over the side. "Dirk," he said, "I'd like you to
understudy Neil's role, and Vicky, you'll be Jane
Ann's understudy. No lead in any of my produc-
tions has ever been sick, but you never know."

Nothing'll keep me from going on, Jane Ann
thought to herself. Still, better Vicky than Phyllis
as understudy.

"It wouldn't be a bad idea to start memorizing
lines," said Mr. Turner, "or at least do a little
reading with each other over the weekend." He let
himself down gently from the apron. "That's it
until Monday then." He dusted off his hands.
"Please push up the seats as you leave."

Phyllis and Dirk left together. Neil followed
them. Lockers banged and voices faded in the hall.
Jane Ann, pretending to organize her pile of
books, lingered as Mr. Turner put on his coat.

"What a load of homework!" he said to her as
he snapped off the rear bank of lights. "Make
sure you spare a couple of minutes for *Our
Town.*"

Jane Ann tried to think of something bright to
say. She was *alone with Mr. Turner. Hugh.* This
was the kind of chance she was always imagining.
Suddenly she felt weak, as if she were going to
pass out from hunger or heat. She struggled with
her jacket, but her arms wouldn't go into the
sleeves. She dropped a book.

"I'll get that," Mr. Turner offered, switching
the full set of lights on again. "You're trying to
manage too much."

"No!" Jane Ann answered louder than she
meant to. Her voice echoed in the empty auditorium. "I've got it," she said. As she reached for
the book her canvas bag fell to the floor. *Stupid,*
she cursed herself. *Onstage I was fine, and now
I'm messing up everything as usual.* Mr. Turner
was coming toward her. "I have it," she insisted.
She put her books down and started all over

again. Getting her arms into the jacket was like some hopeless task in a dream that got more impossible the harder she worked at it.

Mr. Turner stopped and studied her. "Wait a minute—you need help." He walked toward the exit of the auditorium.

Help, Jane Ann repeated under her breath. Would he offer to drive her home? Oh, please—yes! On second thought—no. If he did, she would pass out for sure. She was beyond help. When she looked up, her jacket finally somehow on, Mr. Turner was standing there and with him was Neil.

"I found this character named George out in the hall," Mr. Turner said. "He wants to know if he can carry your books home for you."

Jane Ann smiled, half pleased and half embarrassed. George carrying Emily's books. They were living the scene just the way it was in the play. She had pictured so many times walking with Neil. Now it was coming true. But maybe Mr. Turner had forced Neil.

"Only if he really wants to," she said. It would be awful if Mr. Turner and Neil were just being nice to her because they pitied someone as clumsy and inexperienced as she was. "I didn't realize I had so much stuff," she apologized.

"That's O.K.," Neil said. "I just have my playbook."

"Are you sure . . . ?"

"It's O.K.," Neil insisted.

Jane Ann hoisted the canvas bag over her shoulder.

"So long, Mr. Turner," Neil said. He pushed open the auditorium door.

Jane Ann paused. Mr. Turner had his back to her. "Good-bye," she said softly. She felt a great urge to say something else, to thank him for being director, for getting Neil to help her, for looking poetic on his porch with the smell of leaves and apples in the air, for . . . other things she couldn't even name.

As Mr. Turner glanced over his shoulder, she caught his profile. He looked like the star of an old silent movie. "Good-bye, Jannie," he said. "Have a good weekend."

"I—" Jane Ann, with a rush of courage, faced him. "I love the play," she said quickly. "I love *Our Town.*" Then she spun around and followed Neil.

"Hey, it's dark early," Neil said. The doors of the main entrance closed behind them. A breeze blew across the athletic field from Finn's orchard. Neil waited for Jane Ann to fall in step. She saw his face and his curly hair as a street light went on.

They walked in silence. Jane Ann sighed. Imagining wonderful scenes was so easy and making them come off in real life was so hard. Just now she had barely kept her head with Mr. Turner, and with Neil she was being her usual inexperienced self. She wondered if her horoscope for today said anything about romance.

"The play's going to be good, don't you think?" she asked stiffly.

"Yes."

Neil wasn't too relaxed either, she thought. Probably he was wishing he could escape. Mr. Turner must have begged him to help her with the books. She looked away and kicked dry leaves.

"How come you've got so many books?" Neil said at last, pretending the stack was throwing him off balance.

Jane Ann smiled. Thank heaven he was saying *something.* "I've got to catch up," she said. "I didn't do homework last night because Lydia Haverd and I were—we had to do something—for Rebbie Hellerman."

"Rebbie? Rebbie's a pretty good friend of yours, isn't she?"

"Yes," Jane Ann said cautiously. Was Neil

going to be one of those kids who got a big kick out of making jokes about Rebbie?

"Maybe you can tell me then," he said as they crossed the street. "Rebbie's a smart girl. How come she always goofs off?"

Jane Ann felt better. Neil was interested. He wasn't putting Rebbie down. "Well," she said, "she's got an awful lot of problems. First of all, her mother's—" Jane Ann stopped. "Do you know anything about her mother?"

"Nope," Neil said. "I saw her once at school and she looked like she had a twitch in her face."

They waited for a traffic light to change. "Look," Jane Ann said, "don't repeat what I'm telling you to anyone else, O.K.?" It was a relief to have something to talk to Neil about—especially something he seemed so interested in.

"I won't tell anybody."

"Her mother's—well, I don't like to say it, but almost everyone knows. Her mother's an alcoholic. She's been in the hospital for it. My mother doesn't like me to go to the Hellermans, but I go anyhow because Rebbie's a good friend."

"How does she act—I mean Rebbie's mother?"

"Well," Jane Ann thought back over all the times she had seen Mrs. Hellerman. "*I've* never seen her do anything strange, but the night before last she had sort of a fit. She threw all her clothes in the bathtub. Rebbie had to call their doctor, and they took her to the county hospital. Rebbie got so upset about it, she just wanted to end it all. Neil, *please don't tell anybody.*"

"Are you serious?"

Jane Ann nodded. She wondered if she was building the story up too much. It was probably stretching things a little to say that Rebbie had been about to kill herself. Chances were that the bottle of pills was one of Rebbie's sick jokes. Still, Jane Ann loved the way Neil was listening so carefully, as if she were a famous actress and he was the audience.

"Go on," he urged. "What'd Rebbie do?" They were walking now under rows of oak trees, and Jane Ann heard the tap-tap of acorns hitting the cement. Neil moved closer. "What happened?"

"It was awful," she whispered. "Lydia and I went to her house. We thought Rebbie was dead." Jane Ann paused. Neil was walking exactly even with her. "Then I climbed this shaky ladder, and I saw someone stretched out on the bed. I was sure it was Rebbie—"

"Was it?"

"No, thank heaven, it was just blankets. After that, she came outside. She was safe. And she told us she *almost* swallowed a bottle of pills. There was a whole bunch of empty beer cans next to her bed. And we—and *she* drank some liquor." Jane Ann caught her breath. "If we hadn't come just when we did . . ." She let Neil imagine the rest as they turned off the boulevard and into her street.

"It's lucky you got there in time." Neil's arm bumped against hers. "Sorry," he said. He sounded concerned and friendly. Maybe Neil *had* wanted to walk her home, Jane Ann thought. Maybe he had often wanted to but was too shy to ask on his own.

A gust of wind swirled and a shower of acorns pelted them.

"Watch out for those things," Neil said. As he raised his free arm protectively it brushed against Jane Ann's shoulder. "Are you all right?" he asked.

"Oh, sure!" Jane Ann felt giddy, lightheaded in a nice way. "I love oaks," she said. "I love acorns. I used to collect these very same acorns—from these same trees, I mean—when I was little, and I used to make little baskets and things out of them."

Neil laughed. "Did you ever do this? I used to scoop out the inside with a penknife and make pipes, with a toothpick at one end for a stem. Do you ever wish you were a little kid again?"

Neil's face was expressive now. Jane Ann saw it in the light of the lamppost at the end of her walk. They were home already. Her father's car was parked at the curb. Home already, just when there were finally enough things to say so she didn't have to worry.

"I don't wish I was little," she said. She stopped short and offered to take her books from Neil, but he hung on to them. She leaned against the lamppost and looked across the front yard. "I liked being little," she said. "I had so much fun growing up in this house." Even now she felt good coming home to it, seeing the rolled-up newspaper on the porch, the lights burning in the living room. "But I'm not sorry at all about getting older. I like the way everything is right now."

"Me too," Neil said. "Most of the time, anyway." He looked at her without saying anything, and for a second Jane Ann was afraid of another awkward silence. But Neil rested his hand on the lamppost and smiled. "Want to read lines together sometime this weekend? You know, like Mr. Turner said?"

"Sure!" She laughed.

"What's so funny?"

"I was just picturing you smoking an acorn pipe."

"Yeah," Neil chuckled. "None of that stuff any more though. Now I smoke nothing but cigars."

She laughed.

"Hey, stop cracking up," Neil said. "When do you want to practice?"

"Tomorrow?"

Neil wasn't shy. He was gentle and kind and funny.

She glided up the path to the steps of the front porch. "Tonight I have to see Rebbie." Jane Ann moved up one step. She didn't feel like going inside.

"What time tomorrow?"

"In the afternoon? At two?" She wished she could think of something great to say. Something clever and personal that Neil would consider worth remembering. Even a quote from a play. But her head felt like a balloon. She couldn't think of a single line that was right.

"O.K., two o'clock tomorrow," said Neil. "So long, Emily." He saluted her with the playbook in his hand and turned away.

"So long, George," Jane Ann stood on the porch and watched him go down the walk. *I like the way everything is right now* she whispered over again to herself. At the lamppost Neil waved once more, and then he started jogging. Jane Ann followed him with her eyes until he had disappeared under low-hanging branches of oak trees.

Jane Ann picked up the newspaper from the porch. She couldn't wait to look up her horoscope for today and tomorrow. Neil was coming tomorrow! She opened the door. *I'm home! Where are you, everybody?* she sang inside her head. *Neil walked me home!* Jane Ann dropped newspaper, bag, and books on the couch. The room was deserted. She was used to finding her parents in the living room before supper and Beth tottering around poking her fingers into everything. Now the television set was turned off. The room looked too neat.

"Mom!" she called. "Daddy?"

She heard their voices in the kitchen. From the dining room she saw her mother and father at the kitchen table, so deep in discussion they didn't seem to see or hear her.

Jane Ann stepped into the doorway. "Hi," she said. "I'm home." Her mother and father looked up, both caught in peculiar expressions. Beth tapped across the vinyl floor in new shoes, arms outstretched.

"Hi!" Her mother smiled.

"Hi," said Jane Ann. "I just finished rehearsal." She hugged Beth and bounced her up and down in her arms. Should she tell them Neil had walked her home? That was the kind of thing Lydia would tell her mother right away. Maybe she'd work up to it gradually. *Neil's coming to-morrow!* she felt like shouting.

"How was rehearsal?" Her mother asked. There was something distant about her voice.

"Fine. Great. Afterward . . ." she trailed off. Her mother wasn't listening. Her parents were exchanging one of those private looks. *O.K., forget it!* Jane Ann thought. I won't tell personal stuff like Lydia does. I won't tell about rehearsal. I won't even mention Neil!

"Afterward?" her mother repeated distractedly. "What did you say?"

Her father leaned forward. "Jane Ann," he said quietly, "pull up a chair. We have some news."

"News?" She stood still, clutching Beth's fat legs.

"Come on, pull up a chair."

"That's O.K.," she shrugged, staying where she was. "Tell me now. What is it?" Something was peculiar. Her parents were acting so serious.

"You may have noticed," her father folded his hands and studied them carefully, "that I've had a lot on my mind lately—I've been bringing a lot of work home?"

Jane Ann nodded.

"Well, I got a promotion," he said evenly.

"Great! That's great!" The kitchen was silent except for the ticking of the wall clock.

"I'm going to be a manager in January."

"Hey, great!" There was a pause.

"In Moshannon," he said.

Her mother looked up. The two of them waited for her reaction.

"Moshannon?" Jane Ann loosened her hold on Beth. Beth's weight suddenly felt like a rock against her chest. "Moshannon on the way to Pittsburgh?"

Her father nodded.

"How will you get there every day?" Her voice shook, because she thought she knew the answer.

Her mother coughed. Beth wriggled and Jane Ann stooped to let her down. She hid behind Beth, pretending to tie her shoelace.

Her father's eyes met hers. He got up and stood with his hands in his pockets. He looked as if he was coming over to hug her, but he didn't. "We have to move to Moshannon," he said. "The whole family. It's not going to be easy on any of us, because we all love this place. But that's the way it is, Jane Ann. If we find a place to live by then, we're going to leave Windsor at the end of January."

10

That's the way it is. One minute you could be singing to yourself because Neil Delancy walked you home, and the next minute Neil, Mr. Turner, Rebbie and Lydia, Windsor—your whole world— could be swept away like a bunch of acorns. And there you were like a bare oak tree, shivering and alone.

We have to move, her father had said. Some things you couldn't do anything about, Jane Ann was willing to admit—certain kinds of sickness, for instance, or death. But moving? Why did any grown person *have* to move who didn't want to? How could someone like her father let a company—especially a company that sold big, ugly pieces of plumbing equipment—order him around and say where he was supposed to live?

"I'd like to stay in Windsor, too," her father had said at dinner. "I was born here too, you know, and I've lived in this house my whole adult life. But we have no choice."

"Why can't you just say no!" Jane Ann had kicked back her chair and left the table without eating anything, without waiting to hear him explain again about boring things like opportunities and security.

Now she lay flat on her back on the bed. The door of her room was shut, the lights were out, and there was nobody to see her tears. Leaving Windsor as soon as the play was over. At least they weren't going to rob her of playing Emily. But somehow the excitement surrounding the play had faded a little since she'd heard the news about Moshannon. *Our Town* seemed like a play being put on by other kids at some other school. The main fun of being in it would be the praise for everyone when it was over and the memories you could share afterward of all the funny things that happened. But now—now what would she have when the play was over? "Remember Jane Ann Morrow?" the kids would say when they talked about the play afterward, "that kid who moved away to—to—to some little town."

Moshannon. Even the name was ugly to her— just the opposite of a pretty, English-castle name like Windsor. She had never been to Moshannon, but from what she'd heard and what she'd seen riding along the turnpike, the name made her think of coal dust on porch railings and railroad cars loaded with anthracite. "Can't you say you won't go?" she had pleaded. "Yes," her father had answered quietly, "but then they'd never offer me a promotion again."

The phone rang. Jane Ann rolled on her side and tried to cover her ears with the bedspread. Wound up like a mummy, she lay still and listened.

"Jane Ann, it's for you!" Her father's voice

came from downstairs. She curled up and held her breath. "Jane Ann, telephone!"

She didn't move. Footsteps seemed to come up the stairs and then stop. The hall was silent again. It didn't matter who was on the phone. There was no one she wanted to talk to. Not even Neil. She turned onto her stomach and let tears soak into the chenille bedspread. Letting out sobs that came from deep in her lungs, she lay back at last, dry-eyed and exhausted.

The footsteps came back. Jane Ann heard a light knock on the door and saw a wedge of light as it opened slowly.

"May I come in?" Her mother slipped inside and sat on the edge of the bed.

Jane Ann stared straight ahead. She was glad her mother hadn't turned the light on. Nobody, not even her mother, needed to see the tear-stained face marked with ridges from the bedspread. Don't show *anybody* how terrible you feel, she told herself stubbornly. Lydia would have talked it all out with her mother, but *she* wasn't Lydia.

"That was Lydia on the phone," her mother said gently. Jane Ann swallowed and cleared her throat. "I told her you couldn't talk right now," her mother said. "She wants you to meet her over at Rebbie's."

Jane Ann pulled the spread more tightly around her.

"Why don't you go over to the Hellermans' for a little while?" Her mother must really be feeling sorry for her, Jane Ann thought. "Want to go?" she asked again.

Jane Ann lay perfectly still. Maybe this was the time to confess how miserable she felt. Maybe crying openly, telling her mother how she felt about Neil and Mr. Turner, about Rebbie's troubles, and most of all about leaving Windsor—maybe that would make the pain stop. The worst thing that could happen, she remembered telling Rebbie and Lydia in truth-and-consequences, would be losing *all that*. And now it had happened. *Talk it over like Lydia does*, she said to herself. *Let loose, like Rebbie does. Cry, like Mrs. Haverd cried.* She started to speak, but her eyes overflowed. Some actresses could cry beautifully. Jane Ann had a feeling she could cry well on stage, but in a real discussion? How could she explain herself well in the middle of gulping and sniffling? No. She *wouldn't* tell her mother everything. Not *anything*. They were making her move—let them suffer seeing her suffer.

"Jane Ann . . ." Her mother spoke low and self-consciously, as if she were testing a microphone. "We'll all have an adjustment to make— Daddy and me, too. It may be hard at first, but you'll do fine in Moshannon. You always make friends."

"I know." Jane Ann's voice was flat.

"It may take a little while, but you'll have good friends there and good teachers, and you can visit Windsor."

Visit, Jane Ann thought. Come to Windsor and watch everybody going on as usual without her. Come back to see Vicky or Phyllis starring in the play next year. Or to hear gossip about who Neil was walking home with.

"It won't be the same," she said.

"I know." Her mother reached out and patted her. "I know it's hard, Jane Ann," she said. "Maybe you don't think we understand what Windsor means to you, but we do. In some ways it'll be harder for Daddy and me." Her voice sounded tired. "We won't get a chance to meet as many new people as you will at school. But let's look at the good side. Daddy's got a job he's always wanted. Moshannon isn't Windsor, but we'll look for as nice a house as we can find. We have Beth. We have each other. And it won't be forever. Who knows, maybe in a year or two Daddy'll be brought back to Windsor."

"It sounds like we're—things!" she sobbed. *Sent away, brought back!* Jane Ann strained to stop the tears. "Doesn't the company care that they're messing us up? Why can't they make somebody in Moshannon manager there and make Daddy manager here?"

Her mother got up. "That would be perfect, but in real life hardly anything ever is. Nobody who's in Moshannon now can do the job as well as Daddy."

"Can't he work for some other company that's here? If he's so good, they'll take him."

"Daddy's worked for the company fifteen years," her mother said. Now she was sounding like some dried-up person in a rocking chair, Jane Ann thought—somebody who believed you had to keep on doing a thing just because you'd always done it. Forget it! What was the use of talking? They might listen to her to be polite, but nobody was going to change anything. Her parents were almost happy about moving, she thought.

"So why don't you run along to Rebbie's for a while." Her mother prodded her gently.

"Not now." Jane Ann didn't feel like stirring, didn't feel like doing anything she was told to do.

"Daddy'll drive you maybe. I'll ask him." Her mother started to go downstairs.

Trying to please her in unimportant things. That's how they would treat her for a while. But it wouldn't do any good. They wouldn't win her over. "I don't want to go to Rebbie's," she said.

Her mother hesitated. "Come on downstairs, then," she said patiently. "I don't like to see you all alone up here. We've hardly seen your face in the last couple of days."

"I have to do homework," she said. It was a weak excuse on a Friday, but the only one she could think of.

Her mother stood uncertainly at the top of the stairs. "Jane Ann," she said, coming back into the

doorway, "see if you can make the time we have
left in Windsor the best you've ever had here.
Don't mope. Try to enjoy everything here to the
fullest while you have it."

Jane Ann stared blankly. "I'll come down later." Her mother watched her for a minute and
then went away.

Oh, sure. Enjoy Windsor to the fullest! Enjoy
rehearsing with Neil, knowing that this was the
beginning of the end. Enjoy the *last chance ever*
to see Mr. Turner. Enjoy Rebbie and Lydia,
knowing that there wouldn't be any spring with
them, any next year. Jane Ann pulled the pillow
from under the bedspread; burying her face in it,
she let stored-up tears flow again.

Finally she rolled over on her back—empty,
spent. Probably Rebbie had felt this bad—or
worse—last night, she thought. It was strange
how another person's misery seemed like something happening on TV until you'd felt misery
yourself. Suddenly she didn't want to be alone anymore. Misery loves company, the saying went.
But it wasn't her parents' company she wanted.
She felt like talking to Rebbie. Rebbie's nutty
sense of humor was the only thing she could think
of that might cheer her up.

Jane Ann unwound the spread and flicked on
the light. She would call Rebbie and ask if it was
O.K. to come over. Rebbie's mother would be home
by now. Then in the privacy of Rebbie's room,
she'd tell her about Moshannon. Maybe Reb could
even think of something to do about it—some way
to convince her parents not to go.

Oh, for Pete's sake! Why kid herself? There
was nothing anybody could do! Jane Ann threw
herself down on the bed again. It was hopeless.
The move was probably something that had been
fixed in her stars since she was born, if Rebbie
was right about astrology. She rolled off the bed
angrily and looked out the window. The backyard
was dark except for bands of light coming from

the downstairs windows. The sky was filled with stars. Had God made them and everything else, like her parents believed? Or were stupid stars controlling everybody's lives, the way Rebbie said? Maybe there wasn't any plan to the universe at all. Maybe everybody was just running around pretending things were important and trying to stay busy enough to chase the Scary Feeling away. Maybe nothing made sense, maybe the only thing you could do was laugh. Well, at least Rebbie knew how to do that.

Jane Ann turned away from the window, and reaching for the reference book on her desk, she flipped through until she found what she wanted. She opened the bedroom door.

The hall was quiet. Jane Ann pushed buttons on the telephone and heard the familiar tune of Rebbie's number. *Let Rebbie answer,* she thought.

"Hello?" It was Rebbie.

"Leon Czolgosz," Jane Ann said.

"What? Sorry, you must have the wrong—"

"Leon *Czolgosz,*" Jane Ann repeated. "C-Z-O-L-G-O-S-Z, you dope!"

"Jannie!"

Jane Ann took a big breath. "Leon Czolgosz assassinated William McKinley in 1901 at the public reception at the Pan-American Exposition in Buffalo, New York."

"Damn you, I forgot I asked you that! You faked me out! Hey, where are you?"

"Home." Jane Ann's voice broke.

"What's the matter?"

"Something." She paused. "How's your mother?"

"Better. What's with you?"

"Something bad." Jane Ann bit her cheeks to keep control. "Lydia there yet?" she asked.

"She's supposedly coming at eight thirty. Come on over now. What's wrong?"

"You know our agreement—don't quit on each other and all that?"

"Yeah, sure. What's—?"

"I need help. Reb, you there?"

"Yeah, sure I'm here!"

"Reb, I'll be right over."

11

Jane Ann scraped bits of gravel off her soles as she walked up the Hellermans' porch steps. Even though she was alone now, the house didn't look nearly as frightening as it had the night before. Lights were burning in nearly every room, and the *bump, bump* of bass tones, like a giant's heartbeat, came from the downstairs hi-fi.

She rang the bell. The door opened slowly, but no one was there. Jane Ann stepped inside the entrance hall and looked both ways. A puff of smoke came from behind the door.

"This is the ghost of James Buchanan," said a raspy voice, "Pennsylvania's only president. What town was I born in?"

"Moshannon," Jane Ann said.

"Wrong," the voice hissed. "I am doomed to walk the streets of Windsor until you give the correct answer."

"Come on, Reb," Jane Ann said. She grabbed the knob and swung the door shut. Rebbie crouched against the wall.

"Hi," she said. "I was just sneaking a butt." Rebbie dropped the cigarette into the Pepsi bottle in her other hand. "What's up?"

Jane Ann glanced into the living room. "Do you have company?" She could see glasses and an ice bucket on the coffee table.

"Company?" Rebbie said. "Yeah! There's this lady that calls herself my old lady and this man that calls himself my old man who're *visiting* here for a change. They might even stay overnight!"

"Rebbie . . ."

"Oh, don't worry. They can't hear me. They're in the kitchen. My old man's busy giving her this rap about don't throw fur coats in the tub. Come on, Jannie." Rebbie put down the Pepsi bottle and steered her past the living room and up the stairway.

"But how *is* your mother? Shouldn't I say hello to her?" Jane Ann hung back on the bottom stair.

"*Later.* She's entertaining this surprise guest from Chicago—her *husband.* We'll see them later. Let's find a little privacy first." She led Jane Ann up to her room and closed the door.

"Make yourself comfortable," Rebbie said, sprawling across the bottom of the bed. "Lydia'll be here in a little while. Now, Reb to the rescue. What's happening?"

Jane Ann sat on the edge of the bed. "Remember what I said last night was the worst thing?" she asked.

"You said losing me, Lyddy, Hugh, Neil. . . ."

"It happened. I'm losing everything."

"What're you saying?" Rebbie looked at her sideways. "You putting me on?"

Jane Ann shook her head. "I'm leaving Windsor in three months," she said.

"Leaving?" Rebbie screwed up her face. "You're kidding me." She kicked the bottom of Jane Ann's shoe. "What're you kidding me for?"

"I'm not."

"Where're you going?" she laughed nervously. "Taking the show to Broadway?"

"My father's company's sending him to be manager in Moshannon." Jane Ann spoke as if she were reciting lines in a play she didn't like. "The company thinks we should live there. My parents

are going to sell our house. We're going right
after the play is over—at the end of January."

"God damn," Rebbie whispered. "God damn,"
she repeated under her breath. "Tell your father
to kick his stupid bathroom fixtures in their
asses."

"What can I do, Reb?"

"I'm thinking, I'm thinking." The bed creaked
as Rebbie got up. "Damn it all, we'll find a way,"
she said. "Reb to the rescue. Could you—could you
live with a relative maybe?"

"Who? I have no grandmothers any more. My
Aunt Bea—ha!"

"True. Brightburn might drop in all the time."
Rebbie paced back and forth. "You could live with
somebody else—with *me!* No, forget it." Her face
fell. "Your parents'd never let you." She stopped.
"But they might let you live with Lydia. . . .
Anybody'd feel safe leaving a kid in that family—
no smoking, wholesome food, and all that crap.
Ask Lyddy. Her mother'd let you. Her mother
goes wild over helping people."

"For how long though? Until I'm out of high
school?"

"Sure, why not?"

"I'd miss my parents," Jane Ann said, surpris-
ing herself. "I'd miss Beth."

"You'd visit on weekends."

"Yeah . . ." Jane Ann tried to picture it. She
couldn't imagine her parents letting her live away
from home—dropping in weekends.

"Or else," Rebbie said, "we could both take off
together for California, and—"

"Don't be funny," Jane Ann said.

"I'm serious! We could make it the first night
to my brother's school. We could hitch from—"

"Rebbie," Jane Ann said, "cut it out." She buried her face in the pillow. "Really, what am I
going to do?"

Rebbie tapped her forehead. "Ah-so! Hold everything!" She reached for a book on her bureau,

flipped through it, and read a page. "You're not going to worry," she said, "because *you're not moving*."

Jane Ann looked up.

Rebbie handed her the book. *"Astrology and You* by Claire Keating. This is my Bible. You can borrow it if you want. Look, here's you—Pisces, for the end of this year.

'Don't get bogged down by problems this quarter.
They'll solve themselves if you're patient.
The end of the year will find you with a new
outlook.' "

"That doesn't prove anything," Jane Ann said.

"Maybe it means your father's company'll change their crummy minds and send somebody else."

Jane Ann wished she could believe it. "I don't have faith in horoscopes the way you do."

"You would if you knew more about astrology. Take this home with you." She shoved the book at Jane Ann. "Anyway," she said, "you aren't moving. If the stars don't save you, *the Reb* will."

Jane Ann took the book.

A voice boomed from below. "Beck!"

Rebbie stood still and listened. She opened the door a crack. "Yeah?" she hollered.

"Listen, Beck," her father's voice came from the landing halfway down the stairs, "I have to go out for a while—to see a client." His voice and his heavy footsteps came closer. Rebbie opened the door wider.

"Will you keep your mother company downstairs? She shouldn't be alone just now, you know what I mean?" Mr. Hellerman, wearing a trench coat and carrying a hat, stepped inside the room and exhaled cigar smoke.

"Oh, hello there," he said, nodding briefly at Jane Ann.

"Hello." Jane Ann examined Mr. Hellerman

closely. It was only the second or third time she had ever seen him in person. He looked the same in real life as in the photographs on the stairs—important and in a hurry. People said he was a shrewd lawyer. He seemed tired.

"You'll go down for a while, all right?" he said, looking from one to the other. "Just till she gets sleepy, you know what I mean? I've got this appointment—tried to change it, but . . ." he trailed off. Chewing his cigar, Mr. Hellerman turned to go. He paused in the doorway. "Beck, it's stuffier than hell in here—you been smoking cigarettes? Open a window, will you?" he said. He nodded at them again and went downstairs.

"My old man's involved in a big case," Rebbie said when he had gone away. "He makes a lot of money and knows important people—the mayor of Chicago . . ." She watched Jane Ann's reaction. "He's met the President!"

"That's great, Reb."

"Jeez," she said, "I'm sorry about this, just when you're feeling lousy yourself. We'll have to go down for a while. But *don't worry.* I'll figure something out."

"That's O.K., Reb. How is your mother, anyway?"

"She's all right. The doctors are the ones who're nuts. They think she should go away to a private rest home. I know the kind of place they mean—some fancy country club where they'd make her sit around all day playing games with shrinks."

"Well, if the doctors think—"

"Screw doctors! Any kind—regular doctors, shrinks, fakes like Brightburn—they can all go stick their heads in your father's precious fixtures."

"How come you hate them?"

"They nose around your secrets and try to convince you you're nuts so you'll keep paying them. My old man's already paid a fortune and it hasn't done any good. My mother's not going off to play games with shrinks if I can help it." Rebbie turned her face.

She must be imagining it, Jane Ann thought to herself. *Rebbie doesn't cry.*

"Even if she's not a hot-shot mother like Mrs. Haverd and your mother," Rebbie went on in a shaky voice, "it's better having her here than nobody. This place stinks when you're in it all alone. Come on, let's go down."

At the bottom of the stairs, Rebbie nudged her. "Just act like nothing's different," she whispered as they entered the living room.

Mrs. Hellerman sat on one side of the couch with a glass in her hand. Her eyes were closed and her head was tilted back, as if she were thinking of something pleasant and far away. She'd probably been pretty when she was young, Jane Ann thought. Now she was overweight and had dark circles under her eyes. Mrs. Hellerman smiled and took a sip from her glass.

"Here's Jane Ann," Rebbie said as if she were introducing her in a talent show. Rebbie never called her mother by name, Jane Ann noticed— not Mother, or Mom or Mummy.

"Hello, Jane Ann," said Mrs. Hellerman opening her eyes. "Sit down."

"Hello," Jane Ann said. She wasn't sure whether to shake hands, or kiss her, or what, so she just did an embarrassed little bow and sat at the opposite end of the couch still holding the horoscope book. What was Mrs. Hellerman's astrological sign, she wondered. Had her horoscope predicted a life of being in and out of hospitals?

"I hope you're feeling better," Jane Ann said.

"Oh, I'm fine," she laughed. "Rebecca took good care of me this afternoon, didn't you, Beck?"

"You're all better," Rebbie said. "Doesn't she look good?"

Jane Ann nodded, trying not to stare at the tic in the corner of Mrs. Hellerman's mouth.

"My husband had to go out on business," she said with disappointment, as if the four of them had planned an exciting evening together. "He asked me to apologize for him." Jane Ann could tell she was making it up. "Oh, yes," Mrs. Hellerman went on, "Beck always tells me I'm looking good. She's a good girl, isn't she? She does well in school, too, doesn't she?"

"Oh, come on!" Rebbie looked at the ceiling.

Mrs. Hellerman rocked forward, and Rebbie knelt in front of the couch as if to protect her.

"She went to college," Rebbie said proudly.

"Oh?" Jane Ann nodded.

"Yes, and I started law school." Mrs. Hellerman smiled. "I only went one semester though. I wasn't smart enough to keep up with all those men."

"Come on," Rebbie said. "It was harder for girls then. You could've done it easy today."

Mrs. Hellerman held out her glass. "Beck, give me a little, please."

Jane Ann watched Rebbie measure out a small amount from the bottle on the coffee table. She wiped the glass with a paper napkin and handed it over carefully. It was the closest, the most loving, she had ever seen Rebbie to her mother—maybe the closest she had seen her to anybody. Jane Ann looked away quickly.

"I'm tired, Beck," Mrs. Hellerman said, swaying slightly. "How about carrying my things up for me and I'll go to bed now."

"O.K.," Rebbie said. Mrs. Hellerman got up from the couch. Rebbie carried the glass and the bottle.

"Good night," Mrs. Hellerman said to Jane Ann. The thought of escaping to her room seemed to cheer her. "Come see us again soon—sometime when Mr. Hellerman can be here. He likes to know Beck's friends." As she walked to the steps, she stumbled over the edge of the rug.

"I've got you," Rebbie said. "You're O.K. Go

ahead. Hold on to the banister—that's it. I'll be right there." Rebbie came over to Jane Ann on the couch. "Well, what do you think?" she whispered. "She hasn't flipped out, has she?"

Jane Ann hesitated. "No."

"Good! She's not going away. *I* can take care of her." Mrs. Hellerman disappeared at the top of the steps. "Jannie, if Lydia comes, get the door." Rebbie followed her mother.

Halfway up, she hung over the banister and whispered again. "Two things. Man, over my dead body, two things. She's not going to a rest home, and you're not moving away from Windsor." She held up her mother's glass and took a sip. "I'll drink to that!"

12

Jane Ann lay in bed. Birds were squawking in the boxwood trees, and her parents were already up and moving around. After coming home from Rebbie's, she hadn't slept well. She had tossed most of the night, never quite sure if she was awake or asleep. Sometimes it seemed as if she were in Lyddy's four-poster. Once she thought she was in the playhouse in the backyard. Mrs. Hellerman appeared briefly in a dream saying, "It's all right to go to California with my Beck. She's a good girl." And then, toward morning, she was standing in the wings, waiting to go onstage. But she didn't know her lines! She had meant to learn them, but there hadn't been enough time. Mr. Turner was leading her in front of the audience. . . .

That, thank heaven, was only a dream. But the nightmare of moving to Moshannon was real. She had woken up with an unpleasant jolt and the words repeating in her head: *You're leaving, you're leaving.* Nothing could shake off that voice—not the comforting view of the real playhouse, not the sound of Beth's cooing in the next room, and not even Rebbie's promise: *You're not moving.* Rebbie meant well, but what could anyone do? Lydia had agreed that chances were slim Jane Ann's parents would let her stay with someone in Windsor. "I know my mother would let you live with us," Lyddy had said, "but *your* mother . . ."

Jane Ann closed her eyes and managed to deafen herself to the birds, her parents, and the ghostly voice long enough for one sweet daydream. In the dream Mrs. Turner's baby was born—a few months premature. Mrs. Turner was weak and needed help with the baby, so Mr. Turner decided to hire a student. "Jannie, you're the obvious choice," he would say to her. "You're my most mature student and you've had experience with babies."

"I'd love the job," she'd say, "but my family's moving to Moshannon."

"What a shame!" Mr. Turner would answer. "But—how about if you lived with us!"

At the sound of knocking the daydream died.

"Jane Ann . . ." her mother came to the side of her bed. "It's such a nice morning we've decided to take a ride up to Moshannon to look at houses. We're taking Beth. Want to come along?"

Jane Ann didn't answer. Maybe she ought to go—at least then she could express an opinon about where to live. But so what? She didn't care what the house was like. She wasn't going to like it regardless. Let them have the aggravation. Let them tear up their roots here. They talked a lot, but she was the only one in the family who really loved Windsor. She decided to take a chance.

"Mom," she said slowly, "Lydia says I could stay with her."

"Stay with her? You mean tonight? You just—"

"No, I mean when you move."

"Jane Ann . . ." Her mother's tone was just what she had expected. "When *we* move," her mother said patiently, "we'll *all* move. We're a family."

"Just till the end of the school year?" Jane Ann tried. She'd settle for anything.

Her mother shook her head. "Did it ever occur to you that we can't do without you? Now why don't you come with us today?"

"No, I'll stay here."

"Wouldn't you like to see your new school?"

"No."

Her mother looked hurt. "We'll stop somewhere nice for dinner. . . ."

"I have to rehearse," Jane Ann said. She *did* have to rehearse. Neil was coming at two.

"Today?"

"Yes. Neil Delancy's coming over to read lines with me. Mr. Turner told him to." She'd *never* go to Moshannon until they *dragged* her off. They didn't love Windsor. Even though they made a big deal about not being able to get along without her, maybe they didn't even love *her*. If they did, would they be doing this?

"Neil's coming here?" Her mother raised her eyebrows. Probably she was thinking *Alone in the house—that won't look good!* or some other corny old-fashioned thing.

"Yes, he's coming here. Don't you *trust* me?"

"Of course I trust you."

"Except with Rebbie," Jane Ann couldn't help saying. Why couldn't she keep her mouth shut?

"I see you want to be left alone," her mother said. "Maybe you'll be in a better mood by the time we leave." Jane Ann heard her mother taking Beth out of her crib and going downstairs.

After she had gone, Jane Ann lay back in bed.

Maybe she'd stay in bed all morning. There was
nothing to get up for. Rebbie was going to be
home with her mother. Lydia had an art lesson
with Daniel Carlino. Jane Ann reached for Rebbie's astrology book on the bedside table and
turned to her horoscope for the day.

> *Saturday, October 26. Relax in* A.M. *In* P.M.
> *get all those little obligations out of the
> way before enjoying the evening.*

Maybe Neil was going to invite her somewhere.
Then Jane Ann began skimming through the
weeks ahead. She looked up the day of the play.

> *January 21. Success is possible if you keep
> promises.*

Well, she'd be sure not to break any promises.

January 20. Friends hold the key to your success.
January 22. Seek new levels of maturity.

There wasn't much to go on. But today's entry—
Relax in A.M.—that was good advice.

Jane Ann tucked the covers around her and
browsed through *Astrology and You* until she
came to the section that described her.

> *If you are a Pisces, you are creative, a dreamer.*

That was true. She read on.

> *You are deeply attracted to water
> and other liquids.*
> *Too many Pisceans find relief in liquor.*

She'd have to watch that as she got older. Maybe
Mrs. Hellerman was a Pisces and hadn't known
about the Pisces weakness until it was too late. If
everybody knew as much about astrology as Reb-

bie did, Jane Ann thought, it could really help
them in life. Rebbie swore by it, and she was no
dope. There was plenty to learn from *Astrology
and You.* Jane Ann started looking up the personalities of everybody she could think of. Rebbie
was a Leo.

> *The lion is ruler of other animals. When a
> Leo roars, it's best to humor him or her.
> Leos hate boredom.*

There was a lot more, and most of it fitted Rebbie
exactly.

She looked up Lydia's personality under Libra.

> *Librans love people. They are peaceful and
> go around patching up other people's
> arguments.
> Almost invariably good-looking,
> they like harmony of sounds and colors.*

Perfect for Lydia. There *must* be something to astrology. Jane Ann looked up the personalities of
her parents, Beth, and Mr. Turner, who was
Aquarius. She wished she knew what Mrs. Turner's
sign was, to see if they were compatible. When was
Neil's birthday, she wondered. Reading about rul-
ing planets and famous people under each sign,
she fell asleep again and didn't wake up until her
parents came to say good-bye.

Jane Ann got dressed slowly and read over her
lines as she ate a late breakfast. Some of the play
was very funny, but a lot of it was tragic. There
was one character, for instance, who reminded
her of Mrs. Hellerman. He had taken his own life
because he was an unhappy drunk. The end of the
play was strange. Dead people in a graveyard
were able to talk to one another. Most of them
said they hadn't realized how good life was until
it was too late. The worst thing in the whole play
was Emily dying and George sinking to his knees

on her grave. Jane Ann underlined her part in the playbook and started to memorize it.

The ringing of the doorbell caught her off guard. Jane Ann jumped up and looked out the window. It was Neil. She hadn't even combed her hair. Sneaking past the front door to the bathroom, she checked herself all over. Maybe he had come early because he'd been thinking of her constantly and couldn't wait a minute longer. It was going to be awful telling Neil about moving away. Maybe he wouldn't think it was worth it to spend any time on a girl who was leaving town. She opened the door.

"Hi," Neil said. He stood on the doorstep, his playbook rolled up in his jacket pocket. "Which hand?" He held out his closed fists for her to pick between them.

"What do you have?"

"Choose."

Jane Ann tapped his right fist. Neil opened it, and in his palm lay a little pipe carved out of an acorn with a toothpick stem. He gave it to her.

Jane Ann laughed. "That's great! When did you make it?"

"This morning. It's a freshly fallen acorn. No worms in it."

"Come in," Jane Ann said. "Thanks. It's really nice, Neil." The two of them looked at the pipe. All of a sudden Jane Ann was afraid of an embarrassing silence again. "Come into the living room," she said. "Sit down anywhere."

Neil sat on the couch. Jane Ann, holding the pipe tightly in her fist, started to follow him and then changed her mind and sat in the easy chair on the opposite side of the room.

"Shall we start reading lines?" she asked. That way she wouldn't have to worry about what to say.

"I guess so." Neil took off his jacket and leaned back. "I'm in a pretty good mood today," he said.

"My father's buying me equipment to build my own hi-fi from scratch."

"Great!" Jane Ann said. "That must be hard—to do that. Is it for your birthday?" She'd been wondering how to find out.

"No, my birthday was in September," Neil said. "I was fourteen on the tenth. I usually keep it a secret because I'm a little younger than most of my friends."

"So you're a Virgo," she said. "Do you believe in astrology?"

"No."

"Not at all?" Jane Ann was wishing she had sat on the couch. It was pretty ridiculous to be shouting across the room to Neil.

"No. It's superstition. I've read about it, and I know the charts are based on mathematical calculations, but I don't believe it's a true science."

Neil sure sounded as if he knew what he was talking about. Anybody who could build a hi-fi from scratch must know what was a true science and what wasn't.

"Well, I don't think it's a true science either," she said. "I guess you just have to believe it *because you do*, the way most people believe in God. I used to think astrology was a joke, but so many things in my horoscope have been close to what really happened."

"Don't do anything stupid just because your horoscope tells you to."

"I won't." Neil must care about her a little bit if he was worried about her doing something stupid. Jane Ann rubbed the acorn pipe with her thumb. Should she tell him about moving now and see if he got upset? She opened her mouth, but nothing came out. Neil shifted positions on the couch and looked around. "Nobody's home?" he asked.

"No, they went—for a ride." Something was keeping her from telling him about Moshannon.

"So let's start, I guess," he said. Neil unrolled

his playbook. "How about on page thirty? We never got that far before. Start from where George asks Emily to write him a letter when he goes away to college. Where they're sipping sodas through a straw—slurp, slurp."

"Want a soda?" Jane Ann asked. "I mean in real life?"

"Oh, I thought that was your line. Yeah," Neil said, "Sure."

She got up. "Is a Coke O.K.? I'll be right back." Jane Ann took the acorn pipe with her to the kitchen. She wished she had something to give Neil that was as right a present as the pipe was. Maybe someday when she got up enough nerve she'd give him one of the poems she had written to him. She took the Coke out of the refrigerator. They were at the good part of the play. George was going to be saying that he was fond of Emily, and then the two of them would be promising to wait forever for each other. Jane Ann wondered what it would be like at rehearsal when they had to practice the kiss. Phyllis Cooper would die of envy.

"Now you can slurp, slurp for real," she said, as she gave Neil the Coke.

"Thanks," he said. "Why don't you sit here on the couch? I can't even see you all the way over there. George and Emily are supposed to be sitting next to each other."

Jane Ann sat down. Neil, leaning back and sipping his Coke, looked pretty relaxed, she thought, for a kid who was supposed to be shy. The idea of an embarrassed silence didn't even worry her any more. She could always just smile warmly at him. Jane Ann sat down at the opposite end of the couch and put her soda on the end table. As she turned, Neil made a quick movement to the middle cushion, and she felt his arm around her. She opened her eyes wide and then closed them tightly and held her breath. The couch was old, and as Neil put his face close to hers, they both sank deep into the cushions. She felt Neil's cheek—soft as the sofa pillow—against hers, and then she felt a gentle brushing sensation against her lips. Opening her eyes slowly, the first thing she saw was Neil's right arm twisted awkwardly. He was still holding the can of soda.

"Slurp, slurp," he said, "let me put this thing down. Now . . ." He leaned toward her, and while she was still wondering whether he had actually kissed her or whether she had imagined it, Neil put both his arms around her and kissed her again so that this time she knew for sure.

After that, they talked about the play and Mr. Turner and Rebbie's mother. *I'm moving away, Neil*, Jane Ann was on the brink of telling him several times. *Does it matter to you?* But she couldn't get the words out. They read all their lines in the play, and finally, when they came to the wedding scene, they practiced the kiss again.

13

For the first few weeks she knew about it, Jane Ann hadn't told Neil she was moving. She hadn't told anyone except Rebbie and Lydia. Keeping it a secret had been better. Once everyone knew, the move had begun to seem final. By now—January—only Rebbie still expected a miracle. "Be cool," Rebbie kept telling her. "Something's going to happen. Your horoscope's favorable. Trust in the stars."

Jane Ann had made sure to keep a close account of everything as the weeks passed. Sometimes she wrote in her diary when she was alone at night,

and sometimes she unlocked it to jot down a few
sentences at school. Details would matter a lot to
her later, she thought—when she was gone. Study
hall was always a good time to catch up on the
diary.

*Thursday, Jan. 30. Rebbie must be cutting
school. She wasn't in homeroom or English, and
she's not here now. I hope nothing's wrong. Lydia
got excused this morning to work on scenery. I
can't believe it—the play is this weekend! A week
from now I'll be gone.*

Jane Ann stopped writing. Everybody had
known for weeks now that she was moving. The
cast was planning a party for her last night in
Windsor. Phyllis Cooper was being unbearably
nice to her. Jane Ann looked at the clock. Ten
minutes until the bell. Flipping through the diary,
she read over old entries that went all the way
back to October.

*Thursday, Oct. 31 (study hall). It's Halloween.
I just came from history class. Some kids dressed
up to make the other kids guess what historical
figures they were. Rebbie nearly got suspended
for borrowing a wheelchair from the nurse's
room. She sat in the chair and kept saying, "I
hate war. Eleanor hates war. I hate Eleanor."
(She was supposed to be Franklin Delano Roosevelt.)*

*Rebbie went to her special astrology shop yes-
terday and got her complete chart done, and mine,
and her mother's. She says my tenth house rules.
That means a favorable outlook on family affairs.
Rebbie says I'm not going to Moshannon.*

*Wednesday, Nov. 13. Everybody knows. It's
horrible. They keep reminding me about it.
They're all saying, "Gee, do you have to move?"
and "Man, that's a bummer." Neil walked me*

*home after rehearsal, and this is how I finally had to tell him. I should have expected it. When we got to my house the sun was still shining and Neil was holding my hand and I was feeling very peaceful. Then all of a sudden I saw the sign on the lawn—*SOLD. *I broke down, and naturally I had to tell Neil about moving. "I'll come up to Moshannon to visit you," he said right away. I'll be glad if he does, but he annoyed me a little. He sounded cheerful, as if he was glad to have some place to take a trip to.*

Thursday, Nov. 14 (study hall). Mr. Turner told me today that he's very sorry I'm leaving. He'll be sorry to lose me were his exact words. I told him I wished I could find a way to stay here, but he didn't take the hint. Hugh, what if I never see you again? (I'll die if anyone reads this diary.)

Sunday, Nov. 17 (home—in the kitchen). Mom and Daddy went to look at houses again. They're hurt that I don't want to go, but tough on them! I know I'm going to hate Moshannon. Anyway I'm stuck here watching Beth. Actually Beth's getting to be fun. I used to hardly notice her. Now she talks a lot and imitates me. Once I told Neil I liked being our age, but since then I've changed my mind. It would be nice to be a little kid again. For instance, Beth can cry whenever she feels like it and everybody comes running to see what's the matter. And when she cries, it's just for a minute. She forgets her troubles right away.

Saturday, Nov. 23 (home—my room). Went along with Lydia to her art lesson this morning. Lydia told me something I'm not supposed to tell anyone else, not even Rebbie. Lyddy's in love with Daniel Carlino. Naturally she will never tell him, because she doesn't want anything to interfere with his art. Another thing—there was a male

*model in the life class and I wasn't embarrassed
at all. I must be getting more experienced.*

*Monday, Nov. 25 (history class). Rebbie must
be in a bad mood. She just asked me to come to
her house after school, and when I told her I had a
rehearsal, she said, "Thanks a lot. I should've
made my pact with Lydia." Her mood must be because of her mother. She says her mother's been
sitting around all the time not saying anything.*

*Sunday, Dec. 1 (my room). Why are Sunday
nights so sad? My horoscope for today was* Put
trust in a loved one. *Rebbie still says my stars will
save me, but I don't trust them as much as she
does. Neil trusts science. Lydia trusts her parents.
(I used to trust mine until they decided to move.)
Do I trust anything? Most of the time I don't even
trust myself. Maybe that's why I feel sad this
Sunday evening.* P.S. *I trust Mr. Turner.*

The bell rang. Jane Ann locked her diary and
put it in her canvas bag. It was interesting reading back over her diary, even though most of what
she'd written already seemed like letters buried in
a time capsule. She picked up her books and let
herself be pushed along through the crowded hall.

"Hey." Someone tugged her by the belt of her
jeans.

"Cut it out!" Jane Ann turned around. Rebbie
was pulling her down the hall and into the girls'
lavatory. "Where did you come from? What, are
you crazy?" Jane Ann bristled. "What's the matter?"

Rebbie backed her into the corner by the sinks.
"They took my mother," she said.

"Took her? Took her where?"

Rebbie breathed quickly. "To the Mercerville
Rest Home, all the way the hell on the other side
of Mercer's Hill. My old man lied to me," she said.
"My old man lied to me!"

"Rebbie—she's gone, just like that? They didn't tell you first?" Two other girls who had come into the lavatory looked at Rebbie with curiosity.

"My old man lied, and I'm going to do something about it," Rebbie repeated. "You've got to help me. Let's get out of here."

"Where to, Reb?" Jane Ann whispered. "We have to go to gym class."

"Screw gym. Jannie, please—*come with me.*"

Jane Ann hesitated. "O.K. Where?"

"Outside. Away from here."

"Cut school?"

"Just gym class. That student teacher's *relieved* when two less kids show up for that class. Come on."

"I don't know, Reb. I've got to be back for French."

"Please! *Don't quit on me.*" Rebbie's voice shook.

"Let me get my coat."

"Follow me." Rebbie led her through the crowded hall, first to her locker and then out the cafeteria exit.

The air was warm for December. It was almost like the kind of day in spring when they'd buy sandwiches in the cafeteria and eat them down in Finn's orchard. The two of them walked in silence across the front lawn of the school toward Finn's. Not being in school on a school day always made Jane Ann feel uneasy, like in a dream when she was supposed to be somewhere but she couldn't find the place. Still, being out of school made the world seem bigger, full of a lot more possibilities.

"Tell me now," Jane Ann said as soon as they reached the orchard, "exactly what happened?"

Rebbie dropped down under a tree. Jane Ann sat on her books. The bare branches and the breeze reminded her that it was December.

Rebbie looked straight ahead. "For about a month I've been asking my old man, 'It's going to be O.K., isn't it?' My old man's been *home* for a

month—*that* should have given me a clue something was fishy. Dr. Karl's been coming over
pretty much, but that doesn't mean anything. He's
a friend of the family. 'She's better, isn't she?'
I've been asking my old man, and he's been saying, 'Yeah, yeah.'

"Well, this morning I oversleep," Rebbie said.
"My old lady's still sleeping. I'm looking up my
day in *Horoscope* magazine. Anyway, I go down
to the kitchen and there's my old man standing
around at ten o'clock in the morning talking to
Dr. Karl. Dr. Karl's at our house at ten o'clock in
the morning!

"'Dr. Karl and I have decided your mother
should go to Mercerville for a couple of weeks,'
my old man says. 'It's a trial—a new therapy.'"
Rebbie shivered. "At first I talk nice—then, when
I don't get anywhere, 'Screw therapy!' I say.
'Haven't you thrown away enough loot on doctors?'

"'Beck, show some respect!' my old man car-
ries on. 'Where do you come off thinking you're
qualified . . . blah, blah, blah. You watch yourself,' he goes on, 'or I'll send you away to a school
where they teach girls manners!'

"'There aren't any schools like that any more!'
I yell at the old man, and I slam the door and walk
out." Rebbie sniffed.

"You didn't even say good-bye to your
mother?" Jane Ann asked.

"No. I was so damned mad I went berserk. I
was just about to—no, never mind." Rebbie
sucked in her cheeks and looked away.

"What?"

"Skip it. I didn't do it. I wasn't *that* crazy."

"Rebbie—what?"

"Forget it! I went out for a big breakfast, and
then I came to school to find you. Look what I did
though . . ." Rebbie said. "I copped my old man's
car keys when I walked out. Here they are." She
dangled them in front of Jane Ann.

"What'd you do that for? Does he have others?"

"Maybe. But it ought to annoy the hell out of him, at least, when he's ready to leave. By now he's probably found another set and taken my old lady to Mercerville." A bell rang across the field. Gym class was starting without them.

"Rebbie, look. Don't do anything dumb." Jane Ann stood up. "Shouldn't you have stayed home? At least you could've gone along to Mercerville. This way, your mother might think you don't care."

"I don't!" Rebbie's mouth twitched. "I *don't* care!"

"Now you're lying." Jane Ann, hands in her jacket pockets, came close to Rebbie and stood over her. Rebbie was hunched over, her face hidden in her arms.

"Reb . . .?" Jane Ann hesitantly put an arm around Rebbie's shoulder. "Reb, go back to your house," she said. "Maybe they didn't leave yet for Mercerville. You could go along. Your mother'd appreciate that. She's just going for a couple of weeks, your father told you. Go on, I'll explain at school so they'll know why you're not there. I'll tell Mr. Turner."

Rebbie looked up. "You think my old lady might still be home?"

"She might be," Jane Ann said. "She was still asleep when you left, wasn't she?"

"Jannie, come with me. Come to my house with me and see if she's still there."

"Rebbie, I—"

"Forget it then." She buried her face again. "I'm not going back there alone."

"Well, O.K." Jane Ann said. Rebbie needed her, and *she* was worrying about missing French. What difference did it make if she cut French from now on? In two weeks they'd be getting along without her every day in French and in everything else.

Jane Ann picked up her books. Rebbie got up.

Weaving through the naked trees, they crossed the orchard and walked down the boulevard to the Hellerman house.

"The car's still there!" Rebbie said as soon as they turned in the driveway. But when they walked in the kitchen door, the house was quiet.

"That's funny," Rebbie said. At the same time she saw the note on the counter.

Beck—Dr. Karl's driving us to Mercerville in his car. He'll drop me at my office. Hildy has the day off. I'll be back tonight. Make sure you're here.

"From your father?" Jane Ann asked. She was sure it must be, but it seemed strange that he hadn't signed it—strange in the same way as Rebbie's not calling her mother by any name.

Rebbie nodded. She crumpled up the note and threw it in a wide arc toward the wastebasket. *"Make sure you're here*—underlined! So I can get worked over for being disrespectful. Be home so I can get shipped to some ripoff school that in the old days *used* to give diplomas for being polite. Now they give you one even if you're a rude slob like me, because the school needs money."

"Is your father serious? Would he send you away?"

"He did it to my brother, didn't he? And my old lady? Who else is left? What the hell, I don't care." Rebbie laughed unpleasantly. She walked to the refrigerator. "Let him pack me off," she said. *"You* aren't going to be here much longer anyway. Even if your stars save you, hell—you don't need me. You have Neil now."

"Rebbie, I still—" Jane Ann started to say, but Rebbie went on.

"Man, I should've known when I saw those readings this morning. My old lady's said *Make new contacts.* She'll make new contacts all right in that freaked-out place. And mine said *Difficulties may arise. Lose yourself in stimulating activi-*

ties. Ha!" She opened the refrigerator and took out a six-pack of beer. Pulling tabs off two cans, she pushed one toward Jane Ann and tilted the other to her lips. "Cheers, Jannie," she said, cradling the other cans in her arm. "Forget my old lady. Let's go up and listen to some music."

Jane Ann took the beer can and dumbly followed Rebbie up the stairs.

"I got a new album I want you to hear." Rebbie said as they entered her room. "Plus my old favorites. Let's lose ourselves like mad in stimulating activities." She put on a stack of records and turned the stereo up to full volume.

Jane Ann sat on the edge of the bed. She tipped the can and concentrated on keeping the beer from trickling down her chin. The taste wasn't too bad if you were thirsty. She leaned back. It was fun, in a way, missing school. Teachers wouldn't even suspect her of cutting since she'd always been such a straight arrow. And even if the whole school knew—good. Let them be surprised. With only two weeks to go, she had nothing to lose.

Rebbie sprawled on the bare floor and pulled the rest of the tabs off the beer cans. "What the hell," she said. "Now we have to finish these before they go flat. Let's drink to two losers—me and you. You say you're losing everything."

Jane Ann lifted the can. At first the beer made her feel full—as if she'd swallowed water in a swimming pool. Then it made her sleepy. The Janis Joplin record played in the background. As Rebbie read to her out of *Horoscope* magazine, Jane Ann noticed that the brown bottle of pills was still next to the bed. When Rebbie wasn't looking, she read the label. It had Mrs. Hellerman's name on it. Had Rebbie been thinking of taking those pills this morning? Jane Ann considered swiping the bottle, hiding it. But if Rebbie caught her, she might get mad.

The sun had sunk so low they had to turn on

Rebbie's electrified Japanese lanterns. Only then
did Jane Ann realize she had missed French and
music. Rehearsal! Their third-to-last rehearsal.
Get going, she told herself. *Get over to school.* But
when she stood up, she knew she was too dizzy to
make it. Rebbie walked her around the driveway
to clear her head, but it didn't help. Finally Jane
Ann made it home—just in time to get the call
from Lydia.

"Where did you two go today?" Lydia asked her
on the phone. "I already called Rebbie and I
wanted to warn you, too. Brightburn was looking
for you. She knows you both cut. The sex book
came and she knows Rebbie sent it!"

14

"You talk to her. She's supposed to go to a rehearsal tonight."

Jane Ann hid behind the door in the dining
room and strained to hear her mother talking to
her father in the kitchen. Even though she was
steady on her feet now, Jane Ann's head was
hurting and her stomach still felt swollen. She'd
have to fake eating supper or they'd never let her
go to rehearsal.

"Try not to lose your temper, Evie," her father
was saying. "She's under a lot of pressure with
this play, and with the holidays, and moving. . . .
We're *all* tense. In two weeks the whole mess will
be over and we'll be settled."

"I can't help being upset by what Bea said."

Bea! Jane Ann jumped. Brightburn must have

called her aunt and complained about her or Rebbie.

"I'd take what Bea reports with a grain of salt," her father said.

Jane Ann tiptoed out of earshot and into the living room where Beth was sitting in the armchair. Yecch—adults.

"Come here, Bethie," she said. Beth crawled down and ran to her. Jane Ann picked her up and hugged her hard. Little kids were great—they didn't criticize or ask embarrassing questions. You could say anything to them, even the truth. "You know, Beth, when we first get to Moshannon," Jane Ann said, "you'll be the only friend I have?"

"Jane Ann! Bring Beth and come for supper!" her father called from the kitchen.

"Let's go, Bethie," Jane Ann said, tightening her hold. "I love you," she whispered in her ear. It was the first time she ever remembered actually saying those words to anybody. Beth laughed.

Jane Ann carried Beth piggyback into the kitchen and lowered her into the high chair. They all sat down, her mother passed the plates, and they began eating in silence.

"Where were you this afternoon?" Her mother said.

"Rebbie's."

"During school hours?" Her father looked up.

Jane Ann felt her stomach muscles tighten. "Yes," she said defiantly. "Why—did nosy Brightburn call?"

Her mother exchanged a look with her father. "Lydia called here twice. And Neil phoned to see why you weren't at rehearsal."

"Why weren't you?" her father asked.

"I was trying to help Rebbie," Jane Ann said. She already felt the first tears forming in her eye. Was there any point in trying to explain to her parents about Rebbie's troubles? They would be sorry, but they'd say she shouldn't get involved.

"Helping her do what?" Her mother's voice was sharper now. "Helping her mail out books she has no business with in the first place?"

"Books?"

"Books that Rebbie sends to people at the school to embarrass them."

So Brightburn had ratted on Rebbie. Jane Ann stalled, wondering whether to play dumb. She might as well admit knowing about the book. She was terrible at telling lies. "That was a joke," she said weakly.

"A silly one," said Mrs. Morrow. "Sounds just like your friend Rebbie."

"Don't knock Rebbie!" Jane Ann shouted. Beth started banging a spoon on the high-chair tray. Jane Ann's head was pounding.

"What was it Rebbie needed help with?" Mr. Morrow asked.

"She was upset because her mother was taken to Mercerville Rest Home, and Rebbie didn't even know she was going!" The tears spilled over, and Jane Ann didn't make any attempt to hold them back.

Her parents sat watching her. "That's too bad," her mother said quietly.

"What did you do to help?" Mr. Morrow asked.

"Just went to her house," Jane Ann sobbed.

"For four hours?"

"We listened to music . . . and . . ."

"That's all?"

"You don't look well," her mother said. "Did you drink something?"

Jane Ann didn't answer.

"I said, did you drink—" her mother repeated.

"Wait a minute." Her father laid down his fork. "Jane Ann, we've talked to you before about Rebbie and her whole family. We feel very sorry for them and we trust you. So I'm not going to give you a lecture about cutting school or taking a drink, although I don't approve of either of those things at your age. But the main point is this: are you really helping Rebbie if you encourage her to cut class and do other things that aren't good for her?"

Jane Ann tried to ignore a wave of nausea. "I'm helping her if she feels better." She couldn't stop crying. There was her father again with one of his *main points,* and here she was losing another round.

"And are you helping *yourself?*" her mother asked. "That's what I'd like to know. We've always been so proud of you, Jane Ann, but frankly, I don't like hearing from my sister that a guidance counselor has complaints about you."

"What did Brightburn say?"

"*Miss* Brightburn mentioned to Aunt Bea that she's concerned about Rebbie's influence on you."

"Screw Brightburn!"

"That language is exactly what I mean! I've noticed a change in you lately, young lady, and I blame it on Rebbie Hellerman. I know you're going through a difficult time, but that doesn't excuse everything."

"What change?" Jane Ann pushed back her chair. "How have I changed?"

"Arguing and being sarcastic. Not showing any interest in the house in Moshannon or in the family. Running over to Rebbie's whenever you get the chance, or out with Neil, or to that art class of Lydia's."

"Why should I be interested in the family— you're not interested in what happens to me. Otherwise you wouldn't make me go to Moshannon. And you're prejudiced against Rebbie because of her mother!" Jane Ann stood up.

"Now wait a minute," her father said. "We're all tense. Sit down." Jane Ann sat reluctantly on the edge of her chair. "There's no prejudice involved," he went on. "We're judging Rebbie strictly for herself, and my judgment is that she's a mixed-up girl who could be getting you into some things you'd be better off avoiding. Even though you won't be around Rebbie much longer, there will always be a Rebbie wherever you go."

"There *will not!*"

Mrs. Morrow shook her head sadly. "Were you involved in sending this book?" she asked.

"No." Jane Ann felt like saying yes just to annoy them.

"Let's not make too much out of this business about the book," Mr. Morrow said. "Why do you think Rebbie sent it?"

"To be funny," Jane Ann said in a monotone.

"Some sense of humor!" Her mother shoved a spoon in Beth's mouth.

"Well," Mr. Morrow said, folding his arms, "I don't know if it's a good joke or not, but I think you'd be helping your friend a lot more if you said no to her once in a while."

"Maybe I would, if I were going to be around," Jane Ann said angrily as she got up again.

"These are rough times for all of us," her father said as she hesitated in the doorway. "Probably the smartest thing I could say would be 'Go to your room,' but I'm going to say 'Go to your rehearsal.' Missing one rehearsal in a day is enough."

Jane Ann covered her face with her hands. She felt sick—sick from drinking beer and sick of adults—especially Brightburn. Through the spaces between her fingers she could see Beth imitating her. Beth thought she was playing peek-a-boo. Right now she'd give anything to *be* Beth—a little kid with no worries, who thought that if you covered your eyes you were playing a game.

"Do you want to eat something?" her mother asked. Windsor could be in flames, Jane Ann thought, and her mother would still be asking, "Do you want to eat something?" Jane Ann shook her head. The doorbell rang.

"That's Lydia," Jane Ann said. "She's coming by for me to go to rehearsal."

"Jane Ann . . ." Her mother stopped her. "We don't wish any ill to Rebbie—you know that. Just use your head from now on."

Jane Ann pretended not to hear as she opened the door.

"Does the whole school know Brightburn got the book?" Jane Ann asked Lydia. They walked along Windsor Boulevard on their way to rehearsal.

"I don't know about the whole school," Lydia said. "Dirk Wood told me. He was there. He had an appointment with Brightburn. When he went in her office she was opening this package in a plain wrapper. 'Oh, my stars!' she said. Isn't that a typical Brightburn expression?"

"Did she know Rebbie sent it?" Jane Ann asked.

"She must have. Dirk says she tried to call Rebbie's father."

"That's all Rebbie needs," Jane Ann said. They passed under the line of oak trees, now stripped of leaves and acorns. "You know what, Lyddy? Remember the night when Rebbie told us she might swallow pills?"

"Yes."

"She still has that same bottle by her bed. I saw it this afternoon. This morning she told me she almost did something crazy. Do you think she'd do it?"

"I've decided it's a joke," Lydia said. They stopped to wait for a traffic light to change. "I was talking to Mummy about this. She says Rebbie has a great need to be noticed. That's true, isn't it? She does lots of things just to shake people up. If we don't pay attention to her when she says depressing things, maybe she'll stop it."

"But what if she means it?"

"We've known Rebbie for five or six years,

right? She's played millions of jokes and never did anything yet to really hurt anybody, including herself, right? She just does things for attention."

"There could always be a first time."

Lydia nodded. "You know what I think? If she's serious or even if she isn't, she ought to see a psychiatrist."

"She won't. She doesn't believe in them."

"Doesn't believe in them!" Lydia laughed. "That makes psychiatrists sound like Santa Claus. How can Rebbie believe in a horoscope and not in a doctor?"

"She says doctors haven't helped her mother. She says they're nosy. I wouldn't want to go to a psychiatrist," Jane Ann said. "Would you?"

Lydia shrugged. "Why not? I usually talk to my parents, but if there was something I couldn't tell them, I'd go to a psychiatrist or a psychologist. It would be *easier* to tell somebody who's not related to you. They're trained for that."

"I'd hate it. Wouldn't you mind if people found out you were going and they thought you were crazy?"

"Jane Ann! I can't *believe* you! You don't understand!" The lights of the school auditorium shone ahead of them. "Lots of people who aren't crazy go to psychiatrists. In fact—you want to know something?" Lydia stopped her. "I wouldn't tell anyone else this—not because I'm ashamed, just because it's no one else's business—but I'm going to tell you. You remember that day you heard Mummy crying?"

Jane Ann pictured again Mrs. Haverd's swollen face.

"Well, she was upset because she and my father were having problems. I don't know what, exactly, but something pretty bad, I guess."

They headed across the lawn to the auditorium entrance. Dr. and Mrs. Haverd, Jane Ann thought—the perfect couple.

Lydia paused at the door. "They both started

going to a psychiatrist who specializes in marriage counseling," she said. "They go once a week. I was wrong that day when I said Mummy should talk to me. What do I know? A psychiatrist doesn't do magic, Mummy says. You have to work hard at it. And it can be painful, she says—like any doctor. But she believes in it. Now *my* parents aren't crazy, are they?"

"They're the uncraziest people I know," Jane Ann said. She opened the door to the auditorium. "Lyddy, do you really think Rebbie should go to a psychiatrist?"

"Sure, if she's mixed up. *I* would if I felt bad like Rebbies does. I'd *like* to go in fact," Lydia said. "It'd be fun to find out who you are."

"Is that what you find out?" Jane Ann wondered: could a psychiatrist tell her who she was so the Scary Feeling wouldn't come anymore?

"You find out all about yourself, Mummy says. Psychiatrists don't tell you what to do. They help you figure it out yourself."

"So, you think I should stop worrying about Rebbie taking the pills?"

"Yes. You know her weird sense of humor."

"I guess you're right. Want Neil and I to walk you home after rehearsal?"

"You don't have to," Lydia said. "I'm leaving early. I'm going on a trip to the art museum tomorrow with Daniel's class. Jane Ann, he's so wonderful!"

"As wonderful as Mr. Turner? As Neil?"

"As both of them put together!"

"I still don't get it, Jane Ann," Neil said. "Missing the whole afternoon rehearsal. It killed the third act! Why did you have to—"

Jane Ann picked up her coat. "Good night, Mr. Turner," she called. "Come on, Neil, let's go. I explained to Mr. Turner. *He* understood, why can't *you?* I'm telling you I was afraid to let her be by herself."

"Afraid?" Neil looked at her steadily. "You know something," he said. "You said it—I didn't—you're afraid of Rebbie."

"Don't be dumb," Jane Ann said. They walked silently down the aisle toward the exit.

Neil reached for her hand. "You *are* afraid of her a little bit—admit it. You're afraid to say no to her. I'm not knocking you, Jane Ann. I'm just trying to figure it out."

"You're jealous." She was sorry right way that she'd said it.

Neil gripped her hand tightly. "I don't think so." They were under the balcony where the auditorium was dark.

"Jannie?" A voice rose out of the last row. "Hey, Jannie, it's me!"

Jane Ann and Neil stood still. A form slipped along the back, and in the dim light from the hall they saw Rebbie.

Jane Ann jerked her hand away from Neil. "Hi!" she said.

"Hi. Hi, Neil. Hope I'm not interrupting anything," she said sarcastically. "Uh, Jannie, can I see you a minute?"

"Sure."

Neil hesitated, started out the door.

"Neil!" Jane Ann called. "Wait—"

"I'll wait outside."

"Reb, what are you doing here?" Jan Ann whispered. "I thought your father said in the note *Make sure you're home*."

"I sneaked out because this is important and I knew you were here. Brightburn called my old man at the office."

"She knows about—"

"You're damned right. Brightburn knows about the sex book, about me driving and smoking, us cutting, me *leading you astray*—ha! Brightburn knows all. And my old man's given me the word. *No choice*—psychological workup tomorrow at eleven in the guidance office. Interview with shrink, inkblot tests, the whole bit."

"Don't worry, Reb. Lydia's mother believes in psychiatrists."

"She would."

"Everything'll work out all right."

"Yeah, it will, because I'm not going to be there."

"How're you going to get out of it?"

"I'll tell you in the morning. I've been studying my chart and horoscope, and yours too."

"What do they say?"

"Tomorrow's *it* for both of us."

"*It?* In what way? Come on, Reb, cut the secrecy."

"I can't give you details until I see the horoscope in tomorrow morning's paper. I'll meet you in homeroom."

"Sure, but—how's your mother? Did you hear anything yet? Reb? Come with us now. Neil and I will walk you home."

"No." Rebbie, forcing a smile, put her hands in her jacket pocket. "I have a way home." She backed into the hall.

"What do you mean? What way?" Jane Ann followed her. There was a strange look on Rebbie's face.

"These," Rebbie said. She jangled her father's car keys in front of her.

"Hey, Rebbie, come here!" Jane Ann called. But Rebbie had already disappeared.

15

"Did you think I wouldn't show?" Rebbie entered homeroom and sat on the edge of Jane Ann's desk.

"Homeroom began exactly fourteen minutes ago," Mrs. Nolan said stiffly. "Rebbie, you know you're to report to guidance at eleven?"

"I know." Rebbie turned her back on Mrs. Nolan. "Jannie—the girls' lavatory when the bell rings! I've got the horoscopes. The lavatory!"

"Just for a second though," Jane Ann said. She hated to admit it, but in a way she had been hoping Rebbie wouldn't come to school. Things were complicated enough—dress rehearsal at one thirty and Neil being mad at her. At first Neil had been understanding about Rebbie's problems, but now he seemed annoyed. "*Forget* Rebbie for once," he had said to her last night on the way home. And then there was that other dumb remark of his: *You're afraid of Rebbie.*

The bell rang. Jane Ann unconsciously looked for Lydia. She wished Lyddy hadn't gone on the trip with Daniel Carlino's class. She would have been the perfect person to convince Rebbie to go for the workup.

"The girls' john," Rebbie said, nudging her into the hall.

Jane Ann let herself be led. Rebbie, impatient, pulled open the door. They had the lavatory to themselves.

"Jannie," Rebbie said, "we've got to do something. The horoscopes say so." Her hand shook as she took the astrology book and newspaper clippings out of her bulging knapsack.

"What do we have to do?"

Rebbie handed her a clipping with sentences underlined in red. "Now I know what you're going to say, but let me finish first. I've studied this stuff. Stayed up half the night. We've got to take off."

"Take off?" Jane Ann repeated.

"Yeah."

"Are you kidding?" Jane Ann scoffed. "I can't go anywhere. I've got a final rehearsal. I'm in trouble now for cutting yesterday. You're in *worse* trouble. What do you mean, take off?"

Rebbie shifted her weight and clutched the newspaper clipping. "Look, I've got to get to Mercerville before noon, and you've got to come with me. If we don't go, then my mother's finished."

"Finished? What are you talking about?"

"It's out of our hands." Rebbie took her astrological chart out of the knapsack and dropped the sack on the floor. "It's in the stars. The sun in my solar fifth house accentuates parent-child relationships until—"

"Reb, please. I don't know what all that junk means."

"O.K. then, the simple version. *Horoscope* magazine says, 'A.M.: *Loved one at distance may need you.*' It's obviously my old lady. I've got to see her this morning. And my newspaper horoscope for today says"—she held it close—

Operate on that hunch in A.M. *Someone is counting on you. Watch a tendency for things to malfunction. Get away from it all in* P.M.

"My hunch is something's wrong with my old lady. She's counting on me. If I don't get to Mercerville, things will malfunction."

Jane Ann heard the bell ring again. They were late to first period. "Rebbie, I can't believe in horoscopes like you can. Is there anything *real* that makes you think your mother needs you?"

"Yeah. My old man was on the phone late last night. He was talking to somebody about my mother, and he wouldn't tell me what it was about. I'm sure of it. The more I think about it, the surer I am that something's happened to her."

"Can you call the rest home?"

"I tried. Late last night and before school. You get a goddamn recorded announcement."

"But Reb, I can't leave school, and neither can you. You have to go to guidance at eleven. If something serious was wrong, your father would—"

"My father would pretend everything was O.K., like he always does! Or sneak out on me like he did this morning."

"He left without saying anything to you?"

"Yeah. He and I have this terrific, warm relationship, don't we?"

"Go to Mercerville *after* school, Reb. Are you sure you aren't imagining something with your mother just to—well, you know, just to get out of going to the tests?"

"Didn't you hear? Didn't you see the clipping? She needs me in the *morning!*" Rebbie's voice was testy.

"O.K." Jane Ann felt her stomach tighten. It wasn't going to be easy to change Rebbie's mind. "Now even if by some weird chance you're right about your mother," Jane Ann said patiently, "what do you think you can do?"

"Be there."

Jane Ann nodded. She remembered again Rebbie sitting by her mother, pouring the drink, catching her when she stumbled.

"Yeah," Jane Ann considered, "maybe you should go. Even if Brightburn and your father are annoyed, you can always take the tests another day. Go ahead, Reb—you go. I can't. I've got rehearsal."

Rebbie planted her hands on her hips. "Rehearsal's not until later," she said.

"I can't take a chance being late. Hugh said don't let it happen again."

"Not even in a matter of *life and death?*"

"You don't know that for sure." Jane Ann studied Rebbie's expression. *Whose life and death?* She saw a vision of an empty brown bottle. "Whose life and death?" she asked.

"My old lady's! Come with me. Jannie, *please.* I'm scared of what I'll find at Mercerville."

"Reb, I—"

"Remember our agreement," Rebbie said, "never quit on each other. We shook on it." Her eyes narrowed. "Are you quitting?"

"No . . ." Jane Ann tried to think logically, but everything was confused. She had promised to stand by Rebbie. But how was she supposed to know if this was real trouble? *Success is possible if you keep promises.* That was her own horoscope for today in Rebbie's book. *Friends are the key to your sucess.* That was another entry. They might get to the rest home and be sent away. On the other hand, if she refused to go, and Rebbie did something stupid. . . . "How would we get there?" she asked.

"By bus. An hour each way."

"I couldn't make it back for rehearsal at one thirty—no way."

"Yes you could. Buses run all the time. Once we know what's going on, you can turn around and get on the next bus, even if I have to stay."

"Rebbie, it's . . ." *insane* she was about to say, but she stopped herself. "It's a dumb thing to do."

"It's the last favor I'll have a chance to ask you."

That was true, Jane Ann thought. In a week she'd be packing. Nothing could save her now from going to Moshannon. She stood, knocking her knuckles against the cold sink, while a daydream unfolded inside her head: *She and Rebbie*

arriving at Mrs. Hellerman's bedside just in time.
"*Now that you're here she's going to pull through!*" *the doctors would tell them.* "O.K., I'll go," Jane Ann said.

"Jannie . . ." Rebbie's eye were wet. *Rebbie doesn't cry,* Jane Ann had told herself before. But she was crying now.

"I'll never forget this," Rebbie said.

"It's O.K., Reb. Let's go."

"Yecch. Look at the weather." Jane Ann lowered her head and put up her hood as protection against the drizzle. "Walk faster. We don't need Brightburn hauling us in before we get to the bus stop."

"She won't," Rebbie said. "She's too busy lining up shrinks and making inkblots all over the place." They crossed the street. "About the bus," Rebbie said hesitantly, "the best one is on Route 51."

"Route 51!" Jane Ann looked up. "How do we get there? I thought we could get a bus right here on Windsor Boulevard!"

"On Route 51 it's faster. They come every ten minutes. Look," Rebbie said as she detoured off the boulevard into a side street, "you're not going to like this, but it's the quickest."

"What is? Where are you going?"

Rebbie held out her fist and opened it slowly. In her palm was a set of car keys.

"Oh, no you don't, Reb! I'm not . . . That's crummy! You said—"

"Shhhh! Don't bust a gut! Look, the car's right there. I drove to school this morning. We'll just go as far as the bus stop on Route 51. That way we can be sure of getting you back in time."

"Rebbie, I'm not riding in that car with you. I'll go back to school." But Jane Ann knew as she made the threat that she wouldn't keep it.

Rebbie walked to the driver's side. "You're probably thinking, 'She doesn't know which end of a car is up,' but that's not true. I've driven all over with my brother. Even out to Route 51 that day we checked out Hugh's house." She got into the car. "Get in, Jannie." Rebbie reached over and opened the door for her. "Come on!" she called. "Hey, here comes somebody!"

Jane Ann whirled around. A man was walking down the block. Panicking, she ducked into the front seat. "O.K.," she said, "but just drive to your house. Please let's get rid of the car. They can cream you for driving without a license."

Rebbie stared. "You mean you wouldn't take a chance for *your* mother?"

Jane Ann didn't answer. Sure she'd take a chance. But this was different. Rebbie loved chances. Taking a chance was probably the main point.

"Just drop off the car," Jane Ann said.

Rebbie turned the key in the ignition, revved the motor, and put the car in gear. She seemed pretty experienced, Jane Ann had to admit. "It's a Cutlass," Rebbie said. "With power steering. It's a cinch to drive. Want to try later on?"

"No. Hey, this isn't your father's car."

"My mother's. She hasn't driven it in a long time. I hated seeing it wasted. It's a perfectly good car. I put my old man's keys back last night before he even missed them. These I took this morning." Rebbie stopped for a sign, looked both ways, and turned onto the boulevard. "I drive O.K., don't I?" she asked.

"I guess so," Jane Ann said, looking at the maze of gadgets and buttons. "What would your father do if he found out?"

"He'd say, 'Beck, never do that again, or I'll send you off to a school where they teach girls not to steal cars!' "

Jane Ann avoided looking at Rebbie. "We're going to your house, aren't we? To leave off the car?"

Rebbie slowed down at the Mercer Street intersection and turned left. "We're going out to the bus, Jannie. You'll thank me later when you see what good time we make."

They stopped for a traffic light. Jane Ann was silent. She should have been mad at Rebbie, she supposed, for getting her into the car—for getting her into this whole damned trip. But somehow she wasn't mad. It seemed as if fate had taken over. There was nothing she could do about it. It was in the stars. And besides, it was kind of exciting to be on their own, riding out of Windsor without anybody knowing where they were. It would be a good story to tell later—when it was all over.

Jane Ann tried sitting back and relaxing. *I should fasten my seat belt* went through her mind, and she laughed out loud. Here she was, cutting class, riding down Mercer Street in the rain with Rebbie, telling herself to be cool, and the first thing she thought about was fastening a seat belt.

"What's funny?" Rebbie asked.

"Nothing," she said. "Reb, am I too uptight?"

"Yeah, you're a good kid, but you have to watch being a little too square." Rebbie moved to get comfortable at the wheel. She seemed to be enjoying herself now that they were away from school. Even the worry about her mother seemed to have lifted. Could the whole thing about Mrs. Hellerman be a fake?

"You take a lot of stuff too seriously," Rebbie went on. "Schoolwork, for instance."

"I like studying."

"Well, pleasing your parents then. Getting hung up on being a good little girl."

"I've been arguing with them a lot lately."

"You should wing it more on your own."

"I know."

Rebbie pulled out to pass a truck. "And you know, Neil's making you be sort of square."

Jane Ann made a face. "He is not. Hey, slow

down, Reb!" Jane Ann waited until they were back in their lane. "How come you don't like Neil any more?" she asked.

"I like him," Rebbie said. "I like him O.K." She honked and passed another truck. "He's like the Haverds, that's all. I can figure him like I can figure them. He'll go to some smart-ass college where he'll be president of the Ham Radio Club or some damned thing, and he'll work summers at a camp for kids in wheelchairs, and—"

"So? What's wrong with that?"

"That stuff bores me. I'd rather travel. Remember once I mentioned us going to California—as a joke?" Rebbie turned on the car radio and fiddled with the dial.

Keep your eyes on the road, Jane Ann thought to herself.

"We could go, you know," Rebbie said softly.

"Oh, cut it out."

"We could. Just get on Route 80 West and fly. I know where to get on. You wouldn't have to go to Moshannon ever."

"Rebbie, don't be an imbecile. I have to be back in a couple of hours. Hey, where's the bus stop?" The cars coming toward them, Jane Ann noticed, had their headlights on. "Reb, there's the sign to Route 51! On your side!"

Rebbie swerved to the left. "Lucky you saw it. I only drove out here once. Remember when we went to Hugh's on bicycles?"

"Reb, *where's the bus stop?*"

"I think that was it back there. Jannie, look, believe me—don't think I had this in mind from the start. I'm not trying to trick you. But now that we're on Route 51, let me keep going, please? It'll be hell standing in the drizzle waiting for a bus, and then I'll have to come back here for the car later. Please? I'm driving O.K., right?"

Jane Ann stared at the oncoming headlights. She had known in some unconscious way from the minute she stepped into the car that she'd given herself up. Driving without a licence two miles, thirty miles—what was the difference? Why *was* she riding in the rain in a car with Rebbie, anyhow?—because the horoscope said Mrs. Hellerman was dying? Because she was afraid to say no to somebody who might swallow pills? Because she couldn't stand to break a promise? Because admitting the trip was crazy would mean that Rebbie was crazy? Or because it was fun? Because she wanted to ride on and on along Route 80 and never come back? She didn't know the answer.

"Yeah, you're driving O.K.," Jane Ann said. "Go ahead. Keep going."

16

Rebbie hunched over the steering wheel and watched the road signs. MERCERVILLE, 27 MILES. A tractor trailer slowed traffic ahead of them.

"Move it, buddy," Rebbie said, shaking her fist.

"Don't pass, Reb. It's getting foggy. The road's slippery."

"It's taking forever up this hill!"

"Who cares?"

"You're lucky," Rebbie said. "You're never in a rush to get to the next place."

"You should enjoy every minute of life," Jane Ann said. That theme of *Our Town* had never seemed more true to her than now. *The play.* If anything delayed them, there was the chance she wouldn't make it back by the one thirty rehearsal. Would Neil be worried, or would he be even more angry than last night? Maybe they'd send Vicky

onstage in her place. *Over her dead body.* Still,
while she was here in the car she might as well
try enjoying every minute. They sped down the
hill. Rebbie passed the tractor trailer.

"You know where we are?" Jane Ann asked.

"Yeah. Hugh's hill. There's the turnoff for his
house. Do you still love him?" Rebbie asked. Her
voice was free of mockery.

"I guess so," Jane Ann said. "I still get shaky if
I'm alone with him. When he's on cafteria duty I
can't eat anything but Jell-o."

"Man, I wish that'd happen to me. Maybe I'd
lose a couple of pounds. It must be cool to be in
love with somebody." Rebbie wiped the inside of
the windshield with the back of her hand. "All
steamed up," she said.

Jane Ann looked back toward the dirt road that
led to Mr. Turner's.

"I guess some people would say it's just a crush
I have on Hugh and on Neil. . . ." She settled
back and let her mind wander. It was nice riding
along talking to Rebbie. Brightburn, Moshannon—even rehearsal—they were all getting dim
now. It was as if the two of them were going
somewhere just for the fun of it. "Is there anybody," Jane Ann said, "I mean is there anybody
you love?"

"Are you kidding?" Rebbie, driving one-
handed, slapped her thigh. "That would be a
howl."

"Why?"

"Can't you picture people going hysterical? If I
loved somebody?"

"Why? Who'd laugh?"

"Everybody! The poor person I loved, mostly.
Guess who's in love? they'd say. Rebbie! Rebbie
the fat kid? The one who's freaked on the Presidents? Yeah! The one whose old lady's a . . ."
Rebbie broke off suddenly.

"Reb, you're so stupid. That's not what people
would say."

Rebbie glanced at Jane Ann and then kept her eyes on the road again. "Don't give me any polite bullshit because we're friends," she said. "Everybody's always thought I was an oddball since fourth grade—admit it. Remember the dance of the snowflakes?" she said. "Me hamming up the Christmas assembly because nobody was the right size to be my partner?"

"That's when we got to be friends—you, me, and Lyddy."

"Yeah. You finally convinced old Hertz that the two of you together could be my partner. And afterward, my old lady tripping and falling in the auditorium? What a crock!"

Jane Ann smiled remembering Rebbie in the white net costume that stuck straight out at the hips. "Was that the year we started calling you 'Rebbie'?"

"Yeah. Hertz called me 'rebel' and everybody turned it into 'Rebbie.' I hated her."

The car hesitated on an incline. "Do you hear a strange sound?" Jane Ann asked. "A knocking?"

"Must be because of the hill. Motor has to work harder. It's nothing." Rebbie put her foot down harder on the gas. "I'll tell you who I liked," she went on. "I liked Zoller. Remember Miss Zoller? One day she asks the class, 'Does anybody know which President had wooden false teeth?' I yelled out, 'George Washington!' It was the only fact I remembered from the whole goddam Revolutionary War period. She said, 'Very good!' and after that, whenever there was something about Presidents, she'd say, 'Ask Rebecca.' Hey, look at that fog. How does that poem go that Hugh loves?"

"Something like 'fog creeps in on little cat feet'."

"This fog's creeping on elephant feet." Rebbie moved in close behind the car ahead of her. "Where's Lyddy today?" she asked.

"She went to the art museum with Daniel Carlino's class."

Rebbie concentrated on watching the taillights. "She's in love with Daniel Carlino, isn't she?"

Jane Ann bit the inside of her cheeks. Lydia had asked her not to tell anyone. "I don't know," she said.

"Yes you do. She loves him."

"Maybe."

"Everybody loves somebody," Rebbie said brightly as if it were a song title.

"Even you do," Jane Ann said.

"Who?"

"Well, your mother—"

"Hell, just about everybody loves their mother."

"You think about yours a lot. That's why we're here right now, isn't it? You love other people, too. That night we made the pact you said you cared about Lyddy and me."

"*Cared about*—big deal."

"That's like love."

"It's different. You're not going to get me to say I *love* you and Lyddy. What do you think I am, a pervert?"

"Don't be dumb. There're lots of kinds of love. I love Neil in one way and Mr. Turner in another way."

"I don't love anybody any way," Rebbie said. She moved into the left lane as they reached the crest of another hill.

"Hey, Reb, not so fast. Look at the fog in the valley!"

"Jeez," she said, "it's getting worse." A grayish-white cloud blew down on them. Rebbie braked hard and turned on the windshield wipers. "Is there a car on your side?"

"If you can't tell, you shouldn't be driving, dumbbell!" Jane Ann was surprised by the loudness of her voice.

"Let's hope there isn't—here goes!" Rebbie swung into the right lane.

Jane Ann held her breath. "For Pete's sake,

Reb, pull off!" She braced herself against the dashboard. The slashed white line on the road disappeared. The single pair of red taillights that had been a marker ahead of them was swallowed up.

Gray silence insulated them, and Jane Ann felt the spirit of *Enjoy every minute* draining out of her fast. The car moved slowly, jerkily, and at each advance Jane Ann waited for the sound of metal on metal. "Reb, please pull over!"

"Don't be chicken," she said idly. "Open the window. Maybe that'll clear things up."

Jane Ann rolled the window down, and dampness seeped in around them. A car swished past on the left. "Wasn't that guy close?" she asked.

"Who could see?" Rebbie rubbed the windshield again, but the fog was like cotton wadding pressed against the glass. They heard the sound of a siren in the distance.

"You have to admit this is a kick." Sweat stood out on Rebbie's forehead, but she was smiling. She strained at the wheel, down to ten miles an hour now.

"It's no kick," Jane Ann said. "Get off the road!" She sat on the edge of the seat.

Rebbie, laughing, pushed on into the pillow of fog. "Don't you like flirting with death, as the saying goes?"

"No, it stinks. I like living!" Jane Ann fumed. Her stomach was rumbling. She couldn't breathe right. Friendship and promises were important, but there were limits. Let Rebbie keep pills by her own damned bed. Let her mess around with her own life—but leave other people out of it. Jane Ann was afraid she would lose control and scream. She heard the sound of the motor catching again. "Get the hell off the road!" she exploded.

"Well, if that's the way you feel about it," Rebbie said, "be my guest!" She spun the steering wheel and Jane Ann heard the crunch of gravel under the tires. They passed a roadside phone booth dimly outlined in the haze. Rebbie slammed her foot on the brake so that the car rocked in place before it stopped. "We're here!" she said, turning off the ignition. "Middle of nowhere! Now what?" She opened the window and a new wave of mist blew in. "Hey, I can see up ahead. Let me go on. This is a bummer—being stranded out here."

"Wait!"

"I'm just warming up the motor. Take it easy." Rebbie turned the key. The car chugged, lurched forward, and stopped. She fiddled with the ignition. The motor turned over and roared. Rebbie moved along the shoulder. "Come on, let me keep going."

"No!"

They heard the hum of truck tires, and the tractor trailer that they had met earlier passed them. "I'm getting in back of that big mother," Rebbie said. "It's easy to see it in the fog."

"Don't!" Jane Ann reached for the steering wheel.

Rebbie stepped on the gas. The motor sputtered and died out. She turned the key again but all they heard was a choking sound.

"Why's it doing that?" Jane Ann asked.

"Something's wrong—the battery maybe." Rebbie clicked the key on and off.

"You said you *knew* which end was up!" Jane Ann turned away from her. This was all they needed. So long, rehearsal. Hello, cops.

Rebbie turned the key in the ignition once more and put her foot on the gas pedal. "Oh, my God," she said under her breath. "Oh, my God . . ." Jane Ann looked at her. Rebbie lowered her head and beat her fists on the steering wheel. Before the motor died out completely, Jane Ann saw that the needle of the gas gauge was vibrating on empty.

Rebbie, smiling vacantly, hummed to herself.

"Cut the singing!" Jane Ann yelled angrily. "What do we do now?"

"Cool it—you're such a nag," Rebbie said.

"I want to get back! I don't want to get caught here by some cop. And what about your mother? I thought you were in such a hurry to get to your mother."

"I am, I am. We'll walk to a gas station and—"

"Won't they think it's a little strange, these two kids coming in—"

"I look old enough to have a license."

"Where's the gas station? How much money do you have?"

Rebbie was silent.

"I said how much money do you have?"

"Two hundred seventy dollars."

"What?"

"You heard me."

"What for?"

"Emergencies."

"Where'd you get it?"

"It's mine, don't worry."

"I don't believe you have it. Let me see it."

Rebbie felt at her feet. She knelt and leaned over into the back seat. Then she got out of the car, pushed the seat forward, and checked the rear floor. "Ah-so," she said with artificial self-control. "No knapsack." She got back in. "Knapsack is—knapsack is on floor of girls' john."

"Rebbie!" Jane Ann covered her face and sank low in her seat.

"You got any money? Jannie?"

Jane Ann looked out the window. A fine mist was still blowing across the field on their right, but it seemed to be rising slowly. English class must be going on right now, she thought, and after that study hall, and lunch and rehearsal. "Sixty cents," she said. "Lunch money." She wished she were Beth, free to cry.

"So we'll find a station with a sixty-cent special."

"Don't joke. I'm sick of it. Why'd you bring all that money, anyway? Or was that just a joke too?"

"No! No joke. Some light-fingered kid probably knows by now that that was no joke. I thought we might need it."

"To go to Mercerville?"

"If we went on from there."

"Why would we do that?" Jane Ann pretended to be dense.

"If my old lady was O.K. and we felt like celebrating."

"Come off it." Jane Ann opened the car door. "You know I have to get back. This is your idea of a laugh, isn't it, to trick me into coming out here." She closed her eyes tightly, but tears started coming anyway.

"I'm not laughing," Rebbie said. "Hey, don't get out. Look at me, am I laughing?"

"Maybe not out loud, but you're laughing inside. You're thinking, 'Well, I conned that dumb kid one more time!' "

"Look, I wasn't trying to con you. I told you I'd never forget it that you came along, and I won't. But we're not there yet. I'm still going to get to my mother."

"How?"

"I'm going to hitch. Come with me."

"No! Forget it! I'll walk home if I have to—it must be about eight or nine miles—but I'm not hitching either direction. I'm going back."

"Jannie, my old lady, the horoscope! It says get there in the A.M.!"

"Count me out. I don't think you even believe that stuff yourself. You wanted some big adventure. You wanted to get away from Brightburn. I'm going back." Jane Ann got out of the car.

"So . . ." Rebbie opened the door on the other side and caught up with her as she walked away from the car. "Thanks! Thanks a lot—for breaking the pact."

"I'm not breaking it." Jane Ann kept on walking in the mist. "I promised to help you if you really needed it, but you haven't been straight with me. Your mother isn't on her deathbed. You made that up. It was stupid to come out here. Neil warned me once, 'Don't do anything stupid just because your horoscope says so.' I made a promise to him, too."

"You mean promises to Neil are more important than a promise to me," Rebbie said.

"No, but Neil doesn't take cars and two hundred seventy dollars and drag me off in the fog. Neil's not *crazy*!" Jane Ann was sorry as soon as she'd said it.

Rebbie, her face set in an ironic smile, stopped walking. "*Crazy?* Well, what do you expect?" she said coolly. "I'm a chip off the old lady—aren't I?" She looked at Jane Ann with contempt. "You straight arrow. Square! Fink! Go ahead. Go back to your precious rehearsal. Give Hugh and Neil a great big kiss and tell them it was all my fault you're late. Go on! Goddam copout pact-breaker!" Then emptied of words, she sank down in the wet grass at the side of the road.

Jane Ann watched Rebbie's body heave. *Go. Take off*, one part of her said. *Worry about yourself*. Jane Ann took a step closer. "Reb?"

"Don't run out on me," Rebbie said softly.

"Then get up, it's wet there." Jane Ann took her firmly by the arm and pulled her up. Their eyes met. "Don't *you* run out on *me*. I'm going back and you are too."

Jane Ann was surprised at the force of her own voice. Rebbie seemed to be watching her and waiting for orders. Maybe her father had been right that Rebbie wanted her to take charge, wanted her to say no.

"I've got to tell you some things," Jane Ann said. Her breath was short. Her stomach was tight and nervous, but she felt confident. A couple of things had to be settled with Rebbie right now.

"This is a heck of a place to make a speech." Jane Ann held out her hand and felt moisture condensing on it. Rebbie stood quietly, her face red and streaked.

"I didn't want to come here," Jane Ann said. "I didn't want to get in the car, but I knew I would. You were pulling me like you had a magnet. You've done that lots of times." She watched Rebbie closely. "Lots of times I haven't wanted to do a certain thing, but I say, 'O.K., I feel sorry for Rebbie,' or, 'What will Rebbie do if I say no?' Last night Neil said something to me. He said, 'You're *afraid* of Rebbie,' and I told him he was nuts. But you know, maybe he was a little bit right. You have this magnet in you that can attract in a good way but sometimes in bad way."

Rebbie was looking at the ground.

"Reb," Jane Ann caught her breath. "I still want to be your friend, but not because I feel sorry for you or because I'm afraid of you. If that's all there was, our friendship would be lousy. But it's not. It's a great friendship. I'm sorry about what I said before. You do weird things sometimes, but you're not crazy. If I don't go to Mercerville or to California, it's not because I'm copping out. It's because I care about myself and you. I don't want to get mashed by a trailer truck or picked up by some lunatic, and I don't want you to either. I like living!"

Rebbie nodded slowly.

Jane Ann took a deep breath. "You act like you hate living sometimes, but I don't believe it. You say you don't love anybody, but *you lie!* You care about Lyddy and me and about your mother, even if you don't call it love. So even if that's all you have—three people—you still have something."

There was silence. No cars passed. The mist had almost disappeared.

"I don't really have my old lady," Rebbie said tonelessly. "And you're going next week."

"I'll visit, Reb, and you'll come to see me. And you've got Lydia. She cares an awful lot about you. Look, there's a telephone up ahead. Let's phone somebody to get help."

"You phone for help. I'll hitch to Mercerville alone."

"Don't."

"Why not?"

"Because I don't want anything to happen to you."

Rebbie shrugged. "What difference does it make?"

Jane Ann fixed a look on her that forced her to look back. "Because *I love you.* And that's only the second time I've ever said that out loud to anybody," she rushed on. "Maybe if I keep getting experience, someday I'll be going around telling the whole world I love them."

Rebbie stared at her. "Who would we phone?"

"Neil." Jane Ann waited, but Rebbie didn't object. "By now it's third period," she said, "and he'll be answering the telephone in the English office. Neil's smart about stuff like this. I'll ask him what to do about leaving the car and getting back. You want to wait here?"

"O.K."

Jane Ann ran to the phone booth. As she deposited a coin and listened for the ring, she saw Rebbie sit down by the side of the road. And five minutes later she returned to her there—after the call that had shocked like a chain collision in the fog.

"Neil?" she had breathed easier when she heard his voice. "It's Jane Ann. Don't be mad. I called because we're in some trouble."

"Where are you?"

"On Route 51."

"Wait a second. Jane Ann, is Rebbie with you? Everybody's looking for Rebbie. There was a call—they found her bag. Jane Ann, let me put Mr. Turner on."

"Mr. Turner?"

"He'll explain. . . ."

She waited while the receiver made a clunking noise and voices spoke in low tones.

"Jannie? Mr. Turner. Hi."

Jane Ann's throat was dry and contracted.

"Is Rebbie with you?"

"Yes."

"In a minute I want you to tell me exactly where you are, and then I want to stay there until I come. It's extremely important that we find you right away."

"Is it because of Rebbie missing the tests?"

"No. Jannie, listen carefully. A call came here to the school during first period from Dr. Karl— the Hellermans' doctor. Miss Brightburn's been trying to locate Rebbie, and she asked me to help. Something unfortunate's happened, and I'd like you to keep it from Rebbie if you can so that Dr. Karl can tell her."

Jane Ann's stomach felt like melted wax. She cleared her throat. "Mrs. Hellerman . . .? Did something happen to Mrs. Hellerman?"

"No," Mr. Turner said. "No, she's all right. Rebbie's father died of a heart attack at eight o'clock this morning."

17

Jane Ann, sitting on the couch in Mr. Turner's living room, watched the tears run down Rebbie's face. *Keep it from Rebbie if you can,* Mr. Turner had told Jane Ann on the phone. But she had decided she couldn't.

"Your father died this morning," she had blurted out on Route 51, with the last bit of fog rising eerily so that they seemed to be alone in the world after an atomic explosion.

"My father?" Rebbie had repeated in disbelief. "Says who? What happened?"

"A heart attack," Jane Ann had told her. "Mr. Turner said to let Dr. Karl tell you. They're on their way here."

"Mr. Turner's coming here? Dr. Karl?"

Rebbie hadn't cried at all as they'd stood at the side of the road, and she hadn't cried when Dr. Karl had told her the details, as Mr. Turner drove them to his house. Now Rebbie was sitting in the rocking chair, and Mr. Turner and Dr. Karl were in the kitchen making coffee, tea, and phone calls. After all the daydreams, Jane Ann thought, here she was in Mr. Turner's living room at the end of a trail that seemed more unbelievable than any dream. Who said people and happenings could be predicted?

"Want anything, Reb?" she asked.

Rebbie, shaking her head, blotted her face with her sleeve. "I've always *expected* my old lady to die," she said, "and then he's the one. It's harder in a way."

"What?"

"Having somebody close die, who you didn't love." Rebbie kept up an even rhythm with the rocking chair. "I keep thinking, maybe I would have gotten to love him, but now it's too late. And another thing I think: Maybe it was my fault! Maybe he got the heart attack from worrying about the stuff I've done."

"Don't knock yourself, Reb. Dr. Karl says your father wasn't supposed to drink or smoke, but he did anyway." Jane Ann got up and walked to the window. "Do you think it was in the stars—your father, I mean?"

"Don't ask me." Rebbie's chair creaked on the hardwood floor. "I did believe in the stars, but man, what good are they if you don't interpret them right? My hunch—remember my brilliant hunch that my old lady was sick? And all the time the telephone call was about *him*. Him telling Dr. Karl he was having pains."

Jane Ann nodded.

"Why didn't he tell *me* he was having pains?" The rocker creaked louder. "Why did he drive himself to the hospital this morning? I could've called an ambulance!" Rebbie stopped rocking. "If I hadn't taken his car last night, if I'd stayed home, I would've noticed he was sick."

"Reb, Dr. Karl says you couldn't have done anything."

"I could have." Rebbie buried her face. "I'm such a crud, such a slob. No wonder he took off all the time."

Jane Ann walked to the rocking chair and touched her gently on the shoulder. "He loved you, Reb."

Wiping her face with the back of her hand, Rebbie sat up. "I guess you can't help it, but you see everything rosy. You love people and they love you back, so you think that's how everybody is. They aren't. My old man was like me—he didn't love anybody. He loved politics, and money, and

cigars. It's just like him to die—to take off for
good without saying good-bye."

"You're feeling bad now, Reb," Jane Ann said.
"But later—"

"Tea or coffee, Rebbie?" Mr. Turner came in
from the kitchen. "And what about you, Jannie?"

"Coffee," Rebbie said.

"Tea, please. Can I help?" Jane Ann asked.

"Fine. Fix tea for you and me. See the cups out
there?" Mr. Turner handed a cup of coffee to
Rebbie.

"Dr. Karl telephoned Mercerville," he said to
her. "They're expecting him. He's going to drive
you there in your mother's car. I'll get him some
gasoline."

"Then what—when we get to Mercerville?"
Rebbie asked.

"Dr. Karl will tell her, and the two of you will
bring your mother home. He thinks she should try
it at home—see how it goes." Mr. Turner pulled
up a footstool. Jane Ann came in with the tea.

"How do you feel?" Mr. Turner asked Rebbie.

"All right," she said. "You're being—" she ges-
tured toward the kitchen "—you and Dr. Karl—
you're doing a lot—I don't deserve it. I helped
mess up my old man."

"No one was to blame," Mr. Turner said. "Your
father knew he had a heart condition. He gave Dr.
Karl instructions for emergencies years ago. You
may not agree with your dad's decision to keep his
condition a secret from the family, but he must
have thought he was doing the best thing."

Dr. Karl came in from the kitchen. "It's amaz-
ing, Beck," he said. "He was in great pain, but he
managed to get to the hospital by himself. Your
dad was a man who was used to being in charge, a
man used to commanding people. Right or wrong,
he did this thing his way, because he didn't want
you to see him helpless. I think I know what
you're feeling. You're saying to yourself, 'He
should have warned me. He should have let me be

there. He deserted me.' All I can say, Beck, is that
he was a hard man to understand. Some people
say a hard man, period, but I don't go along with
that. He loved you, Beck, and he wanted to spare
you."

Rebbie, folding and unfolding her hands,
rocked slowly. "How do you think *she'll* take it?"

"We have to wait and see," said Dr. Karl. "I
think she loved him, so it'll be hard for her. On
the other hand, she was always in the shadow of
your father. You're sharp, Beck—you saw that.
She was one of the people he commanded, and
she's reacted to that in an unhealthy way. Now
that she's not in that position any more, she may
be more free."

"My old lady's free all right." Rebbie laughed
with bitterness. "Freedom means having nothing
left to lose—that's the way the song goes."

"If that's what freedom is," Dr. Karl said, sipping his coffee, "then no person alive is free. Nobody's got nothing left to lose, as long as they're
still breathing. They've still got that last breath.
And your mother's got a lot more than that—
including a certain person sitting right there in
that rocking chair."

Rebbie tipped gently back and forth. "What's
going to happen to me?" she asked in a detached
voice.

"You're going to come with me to get your
mother," Dr. Karl said. "We're going to pick up
your brother at the airport. And the three of you
will do what you can to help me arrange a funeral
on Monday. Then you'll go home and see how
things work out. Your brother will go back to
school, and you, Beck, you personally will have to
face up to a couple of things. I'm talking about
facing up to cutting school, skipping out on ap-
pointments, taking a car, driving without a license. Then there's the matter of that knapsack of
yours. I've got a couple of questions to ask you later about where you were heading with all that

money. Regardless of your reasons, taking the car was wrong, and it can't be dismissed."

Rebbie jiggled her chair nervously. She looked from Mr. Turner to Jane Ann to Dr. Karl. "Will I get sent away?"

Dr. Karl hesitated. "Not now. Not as I see it, anyway. Not if you and your mother can work things out."

"What's the punishment then?" Rebbie was pressing down on her foot with the rocker. "Back to Brightburn and the shrink?"

Dr. Karl set down his cup and folded his arms. "I don't know this Miss Brightburn, but I'd like to see you try therapy outside the school. Therapy is supposed to make you feel better, and I don't think of that as a punishment. If you got the flu, you might come to me for medicine. And if you—"

"And if you start flipping out," Rebbie interrupted, "you run to the shrink and look at inkblots."

Mr. Turner took Rebbie's empty cup. "When you tell them you see George Washington's false teeth in the inkblot," he said, "the psychologist'll be the one to flip out."

"And send me to the nuthouse."

"No," Mr. Turner said heading for the kitchen, "to the White House. Now if everybody's finished, let's get going. Jannie, give me a hand with the other cups please. Aside from everything else, we've got to get the leading lady to rehearsal. We should just make it."

"Get in the car, girls," Dr. Karl said. "Mr. Turner wants me to look for a gasoline container in the garage."

Jane Ann put on her coat and handed Rebbie hers. "Come on, Reb." She took a last look around the living room. On the piano was a photograph of Mrs. Turner that she hadn't noticed before. Mrs. Turner was attractive, Jane Ann thought. But not *that* attractive.

"Go on out to the car," Mr. Turner called from the kitchen. "I'll be right with you."

Jane Ann opened the door for Rebbie, and the two of them stood on the porch where Rebbie had rung the doorbell and ran.

"Remember hiding behind the hedge?" Jane Ann asked.

"Yeah. Man, that seems like a long time ago," Rebbie said. "Everything's changed." She sat down on the coach seat. "Only Lyddy's the same. Only the Happy Haverds never change."

"You're wrong."

"What?"

"I said you're wrong." Jane Ann sat next to her on the bench. "Everybody changes. Nobody's got it made. Maybe Lyddy'll tell you about it sometime."

"Tell me what?" Rebbie asked without interest. She put her hands in her pockets and looked toward the highway. "You know, it would've been fun—getting the hell out of here, taking off for California, forgetting Brightburn and parents and everything."

For a minute Jane Ann let herself imagine it. Leaping the hedge, running down the dirt road, hitching on Route 51. Living peacefully on a beach or on a communal farm. Then she saw another set of images: Mr. Turner and Dr. Karl looking hurt, Neil, her parents, and Rebbie's mother being upset, Vicky Lindstrom going onstage as Emily. . . . She shook her head. "It sounds better than it would turn out."

"Maybe." Rebbie sighed. "Adults have us, don't they? We can't win. Forget about doing what you want until you're eighteen."

"I guess so," Jane Ann said. She saw Mr. Turner getting into the car. He motioned to them, and Jane Ann got up from the bench. "Forget it even then," she said. "There'll be rules until we're ninety."

"Terrific!" Rebbie stood up. "Only seventy-five more years to go!"

Tears were rolling down Rebbie's face again, Jane Ann noticed. It was good she was crying and getting it all out, the way Beth did.

"I'm just telling you one thing," Rebbie said. "When I'm ninety, man, watch out. I'm doing whatever I damn please."

18

"Rebbie, no!" Jane Ann called.

"Don't say no to me," Rebbie said. "I can do whatever I please." Rebbie was drawing the brown bottle closer and closer to her lips.

"Rebbie, don't . . ." Jane Ann begged.

And then she woke up. It was just another one of the dreams that had been haunting her for the past week. Some of them were pleasant, like the one in the middle of the night about Neil kissing her, but some were nightmares. A few nights before she had dreamed she was at Mr. Hellerman's funeral, but when she looked in the coffin, *Mrs.* Hellerman was lying there. In another nightmare she was riding along in the fog, searching for Beth. "Let me out of this car!" she kept shouting. "I've got to find my little sister!"

What did her dreams mean? she wondered. Did everybody dream? Even now—just before the alarm had gone off—she had seen a fuzzy image, an empty brown square. She blinked and sat up. In front of her, leaning against the wall, was the naked bulletin board that she had stripped the day before of all her photographs and souvenirs.

The board was real. This was it, she remembered—her last day in Windsor.

Jane Ann got up and stood by the window. The moving van was aready here, the house already chilly from drafts that blew in as familiar belongings went out. She crawled under the covers again to avoid the chill and to avoid looking at empty rooms. In the last day or two, dishes and knick-knacks had been picked off the shelves, wrapped in newspaper, and placed inside cardboard drums. Closets once crammed with jackets, tennis rackets, and playpens were bare, with dust balls in the corners. Boxes of discarded toys and broken appliances filled the cellarway. The day had come. The moon in her tenth house hadn't done any good. All the stars in the sky hadn't kept the moving van away.

By now, even Rebbie was convinced that the move to Moshannon was real. "You're leaving Saturday?" Rebbie had said to her at the end of Mr. Hellerman's funeral. "I'll come see you off after my *appointment*. There's this new X-rated series starting tomorrow called *Reb Meets the Shrink*."

"You're really going?" Jane Ann asked her.

"Yeah," she nodded. "I decided I don't want to throw clothes in the bathtub when I grow up. By the way," she had whispered to Jane Ann and Lydia as they left the funeral home, "this'll give you something to think about—which President installed the first bathtub in the White House?"

The funeral had been five days ago. Jane Ann had wanted to hold on to those days. They had gone by pleasantly but so quickly. Not that anything special had happened, except for the farewell party. But little things had been important. Her parents had been very proud of her performance in the play and very understanding, even about her going with Rebbie in the car. Lydia had come over every day to help her pack. Neil had

taken her out, to try to keep her in good spirits.
And Rebbie had telephoned.

The farewell party—just last night—already
seemed like another one of her dreams. Everyone
connected with the play had been at Neil's house,
including Mr. Turner, who had brought his wife.
Lydia was there—and Rebbie, even though she
hadn't been in the cast. Rebbie had brought her
record collection, and Neil had finished building
his hi-fi. It was a great party, but why did people
wait until you were going away to really look at
you and tell you good things about yourself? Having the Turners at the party had been exciting
and nerve-racking at the same time. Should she
congratulate them on expecting a baby? Jane Ann
had wished she could stop staring at Mrs. Turner's waistline. And whenever she looked at Mr.
Turner, she was surprised all over again at something he had casually mentioned while driving her
back to rehearsal: he had gone to a psychiatrist!
Everybody ought to go, Jane Ann decided.

"This isn't good-bye, Jannie," Mr. Turner had
said to her when he and his wife left the party.
"You'll write to us, won't you?"

"Sure!" Oh, she'd write. She'd work over letters until they were masterpieces, until Mr.
Turner and his wife would have to stop reading to
catch their breath. Jane Ann had expected to feel
let down when they'd gone, but instead she was
relieved. She didn't have to worry any more about
where to look.

When the Turners left, Jane Ann had overheard Neil and Rebbie arguing. She stiffened as
Rebbie walked away from Neil and brushed by
her.

"Neil Delancy's a fag."

"What?"

Rebbie had pushed on toward the punch bowl.
"He doesn't even know the birthdate of Ruther-
ford B. Hayes."

When everybody had left the party, Neil had walked her home. He hadn't said much until they got to her house.

"I looked up my horoscope for today," he had said at her front door. "It said *A good day for making a romantic gesture.*" Neil had put his arms around her.

"You told me astrology wasn't a true science!" She pretended to push him away.

"Forget science," Neil said, and then he kissed her so that she had dreamed about it later.

Now Jane Ann sat up in bed. Better get dressed, she thought. Rebbie will be coming over—and Lydia. She put one foot on the cold floor. The wind shook her windowpane. In the yard the shutters on the playhouse banged. It was the kind of moment that the Scary Feeling always waited for—an in-between time when nobody else was around and she was trapped in her own thoughts. *O.K., where is it?* She steeled herself, prepared to recite the facts: *I'm Jane Ann Morrow. I live—I used to live—at 814 Oak Street, Windsor, Pennsylvania. . . .* But the Scary Feeling didn't come. Maybe it was like bad news that waited to come until you weren't expecting it. Maybe she had faked it out this time by being ready. Could she have outgrown it for good? It was about time—even the name was stupid and childish—*Scary Feeling!*

"Jane Ann!" She heard her mother call from downstairs. "I'm sending Beth up to you. Put her in her crib so she'll be out of the way of the movers."

Jane Ann put on her jeans and met Beth at the top of the stairs. "O.K., Bethie," she said, "there's no Scary Feeling, is there?" She carried Beth to the crib and settled her with Fuzzball, her favorite toy. Then she went back to her own room and stared out the window. Patches of snow lay like baby blankets over beds where daffodils and peonies would bloom in spring. The playhouse was staying in Windsor. It would be too hard to move it. Jane Ann heard the bedroom door open.

"Get back in that crib!" she called automatically.

"Man, that'd be a sight."

"Rebbie!" Jane Ann jumped. Rebbie stood in the doorway holding out a box of donuts.

"Here," she said. "I barged right in, as usual. Happy moving."

"Thanks a lot." Jane Ann took the box. "Hey, did you go? Did you see the shrink?"

"It was *nothing*," Rebbie said. "I mean, no sweat! He's just this guy who looks like a South American Hugh Turner, only better-looking."

"Yeah? You're lucky, Reb. I wish I could go. What did you do there?"

"Just talked. No inkblots in sight. I mean, just *sat* and talked. Hey, aren't you going to ask me to make myself at home and have a donut?"

"Sure, make yourself at home and have a donut."

"Thanks." Rebbie sat on the end of the bed. "Eighteen varieties," she said. "I got one of each. I'll take the glazed with coconut."

"They're good," Jane Ann said, catching crumbs in her hand. "How's your mother?"

"O.K."

"Is she drinking?" Jane Ann was surprised how easily the question came out—no substitute word—just the question pure and simple.

"Well, she's controlling it so far," Rebbie said. "Dr. Karl convinced her to go to some group. And we've got a new housekeeper who really keeps house."

"You're going to be able to stay home, to go to Windsor High?"

"It looks like it." Rebbie helped herself to another donut. "Anyway," she said, "maybe going away to school wouldn't be bad, especially now that you're moving."

"It'll be good if you have a choice," Jane Ann said. "That's what got me about going to Moshannon—I had no choice. When I first heard about it, I acted like a maniac. I still hate the idea. But when you know a thing is going to happen, you get used to it. How bad can Moshannon be?"

"Pretty bad. If it is, we'll head for California." Rebbie laughed. "I'm just kidding. Who *am* I going to kid around with, though?"

"Lydia," Jane Ann said. "And the shrink! What's his name?"

"Murillo—Dr. Murillo. I already asked him a President question. He looked it up!"

"What else did you talk about?" Jane Ann asked.

"Oh, dreams. . . ."

"Dreams?" Jane Ann repeated. "I had this dream about your mother, Reb. . . ."

"Yeah? What was it?"

"I dreamed . . ." Jane Ann paused. "I dreamed she wasn't drinking anymore."

"Yeah? Terrific. Murillo asked me about my mother. He says, 'Why do you call her your old lady? Is she old?' 'No,' I say, 'but she's a lady!' He talked about my father dying. We even talked about you."

"Me?"

"Yeah. I shouldn't be telling you this. It's confidential—X-rated."

"Then don't tell me."

"See, that's what it is about you! Anybody else would be begging, *'What did you say about me?'* You just say, 'O.K., don't tell me,' and you mean it. You have this very heavy superego."

"I do?"

"Yeah. This built-in thing that makes you say no, tells you when to stop."

"Where did I get it?"

"He says you develop it, from your experiences and your parents and stuff. Guess I'd better get one."

"I'd like to loosen mine up sometimes. Too bad I can't give you some of mine."

"You did, sort of," Rebbie said. "Murillo says I didn't go completely berserk the other day because I value your friendship."

"I value it too, Reb." Jane Ann closed the box of donuts. "You're O.K. now, aren't you? I mean, you got rid of those pills?"

"Pills? You mean these?" Rebbie pulled the brown bottle from her jacket pocket and unscrewed the lid. She dumped a few pastel-colored discs into her hand.

"Rebbie, they're—"

"They aren't pills, jerk. They're Smarties candies—two cents a pack. Want some?" She held out her hand.

Jane Ann shook her head. "Smarties? I saw . . . That's not what was in the bottle before."

"Sure. Smarties. What do you think makes me so cunning?"

"Jane Ann—visitor!" her mother called.

Lydia ran up the stairs. "Jane Ann, your house is so bleak!" Lydia was carrying a bulky carton that she handed to Jane Ann. "I brought you a present. Hi, Rebbie."

"Hi."

"What is it?" Jane Ann lifted the box.

"I made it."

"A Haverd original?" Jane Ann pulled up the flaps. "A sculpture!"

"I tried soldering wire," Lydia said, "like the big one in Duff Hall. Daniel showed me how."

Rebbie laughed. "Is *that* what you do with Daniel Carlino!"

"Lyddy, it's great." Jane Ann stood the sculpture on the bare desk. "It's a figure."

"It's supposed to be a nude," Lydia said, "but very abstract so it won't shock your mother."

"A nude what?" Rebbie asked.

"Person!" Lydia said. "A man!"

"Looks like a nude egg beater to me," said Rebbie. "Isn't he missing something?"

"Reb, it's *art*," Jane Ann told her. "It took Lydia a long time to make it."

"Oh." Rebbie studied it. "Ohhh, *now* I recognize her!"

"Her?" Lydia looked up. "Who?"

"Brightburn! Hey, sorry to break up this terrific threesome, but I've got to split. I've got to go to the airport with my mother. My brother's coming in for the weekend. Dr. Karl got him to sell his car."

"I've got to leave, too, Jane Ann," Lydia said. "I've got a lesson."

"So . . ." Rebbie looked from one of them to the other. "Then this is it, Jannie. I mean this is *it*."

Jane Ann blocked the doorway. "Rebbie, Lydia, don't go yet."

"I've got to," Rebbie said. She put her hands in her pockets. "Look, I'll visit Moshannon soon."

"When?"

"Next weekend? I'll hitch!"

"Rebbie!" Jane Ann groaned. "Hey, do you both have to leave? I can't stand this. I'll come downstairs with you."

"Jane Ann!" Lydia pulled Jane Ann toward her and gave her a hug. "Will you come to visit us in Maine this summer? Mummy and Daddy said you could. You, too, Rebbie."

"I will if my parents let me," Jane Ann agreed. "Lyddy—good-bye! I *hate* saying good-bye!"

"Me, too," Rebbie said, "so let's not say it. Let's just take off for San Francisco right now—the three of us. Hey, what was that thump?"

Beth padded into the hallway. "Bye-bye," she called.

"Oh, it's you, kid." Rebbie gave her a pat. "So long! Hey!" Rebbie backed down the sairs. "You're slipping, Jannie. You're quitting on me."

"What? What do you mean?"

. . . . . .

"You never told me who installed the first bathtub in the White House."

"Oh, Reb, I forgot!" Jane Ann said. "I packed all my reference books. I'll write—I swear I'll write."

Lydia took a step down toward Rebbie. "The first President to install a bathtub in the White House was Millard Fillmore," she said.

"Lyddy!" Jane Ann clapped a hand on her shoulder. "I thought you hated President questions! Reb, is she right?"

"A-plus. Terrific." Rebbie's voice was shrill. "I'll see you, Lyd. See you, Jannie." Rebbie hurried down the steps without looking back. Lydia followed her.

"Good-bye, Rebbie!" Jane Ann called after them. "Good-bye, Lydia!" Jane Ann took Beth's hand and pulled her along to the front bedroom window. She watched until Rebbie and Lydia were out of sight. Then she picked up Beth and hugged her as hard as she could.

ABOUT THE AUTHOR

ROBIN FIDLER BRANCATO grew up in Wyomissing, Pennsylvania, a suburban town which provided inspiration for the setting of her first novel, *Don't Sit Under the Apple Tree*. Her second novel for young people, *Something Left to Lose*, was published the next year, and this was followed, in turn, by *Winning*, an American Library Association notable book for young adults. Ms. Brancato earned a B.A. in creative writing from the University of Pennsylvania and received her M.A. from the City College of New York. For the past ten years, she has taught high school English and journalism in Hackensack, New Jersey. She lives in Teaneck, New Jersey, with her husband, John, and their two sons, Christopher and Gregory.

TEENAGERS FACE LIFE AND LOVE

Choose books filled with fun and adventure, discovery and disenchantment, failure and conquest, triumph and tragedy, life and love.

☐	12033	**THE LATE GREAT ME** Sandra Scoppettone	$1.75
☐	10946	**HOME BEFORE DARK** Sue Ellen Bridgers	$1.50
☐	11961	**THE GOLDEN SHORES OF HEAVEN** Katie Letcher Lyle	$1.50
☐	12501	**PARDON ME, YOU'RE STEPPING ON MY EYEBALL!** Paul Zindel	$1.95
☐	11091	**A HOUSE FOR JONNIE O.** Blossom Elfman	$1.95
☐	12025	**ONE FAT SUMMER** Robert Lipsyte	$1.75
☐	12252	**I KNOW WHY THE CAGED BIRD SINGS** Maya Angelou	$1.95
☐	11800	**ROLL OF THUNDER, HEAR MY CRY** Mildred Taylor	$1.75
☐	12741	**MY DARLING, MY HAMBURGER** Paul Zindel	$1.95
☐	10370	**THE BELL JAR** Sylvia Plath	$1.95
☐	12338	**WHERE THE RED FERN GROWS** Wilson Rawls	$1.75
☐	11829	**CONFESSIONS OF A TEENAGE BABOON** Paul Zindel	$1.95
☐	11632	**MARY WHITE** Caryl Ledner	$1.95
☐	11640	**SOMETHING FOR JOEY** Richard E. Peck	$1.75
☐	12347	**SUMMER OF MY GERMAN SOLDIER** Bette Greene	$1.75
☐	11839	**WINNING** Robin Brancato	$1.75
☐	12057	**IT'S NOT THE END OF THE WORLD** Judy Blume	$1.50